REVENGE

BOOK TWO IN THE VAEDRA CHRONICLES SERIES

ESTER LÓPEZ

Writing & Photographic Services LLC

Published by
Writing & Photographic Services, LLC
REVENGE

ISBN: 978-1-7347536-5-3
2nd Edition July 2020

DEDICATION

For my son, Jason, who is the inspiration for Berto.

ABOUT THE AUTHOR

To keep up to date on the author's book releases, and to get
the FREE "Vaedra Chronicles" companion book, please join
Ester's Readers Group at:
www.esterlopez.com
Follow Ester's blogs at:
www.esterlopez.com
www.authorblogspot.esterlopez.com/
Follow Ester on:
Facebook at Ester Lopez Author
Or on Twitter
@esterlopez1
And if you like the story, please leave an honest review at
your favorite book seller
You can also join Ester's Group Page on Facebook at
Virtual Book Signing & Takeover Group

D*enoy, Planet Tarsius*

Mariposa frowned at Berto. "Did you get in trouble today at the Academy?"

Berto sat by the fire pit, cooking a wild taffit bird on a makeshift spit. He tore off a leg and handed it to his sister. "Don't eat the bones, Mariposa, and no, I didn't get in trouble." He took a bite of taffit. The juices from the succulent bird dripped down his chin. He wiped it off with the back of his hand. He was hungrier than he thought. The sweet aroma of the roasting bird had his stomach growling but the luscious taste made him forget how he had to live.

"I saw you talking to Headmaster Torres." She took a bite of the leg, glancing up at him.

"Headmaster Torres found a job for me. I start tomorrow after classes. I'll learn how to fix wing ships, then maybe cargo ships."

"What about me? Who is going to watch me while you're gone?"

He bowed his head. Seven anos was too young to leave

alone, but he had been orphaned at that age with an infant sister to take care of.

"Promise me you'll stay here in the cave when you get finished with classes."

"Aren't you going to walk me home?" She bit her lower lip and raised her brows.

"Mari, I would, but the job is on the other side of Denoy. I would be late getting to work."

Mari pouted, on the verge of tears.

"Look, Mari, it's only for one day. I'll ask my new boss if you can come with me. You can study while I work."

"Can't I go with you tomorrow?"

"No, Mari. I have to speak to the boss first to make sure it's okay. Now, eat your taffit."

Later, he tucked her into the makeshift bed of reeds and palms with a blanket he had stolen years before. He looked forward to the day he could pay for his food. When he couldn't catch anything to eat, he'd stolen it.

He washed up by the small waterfall that trickled into a shallow pool. The coolness of the cave and the smell of wet rock was constant and kept out the heat of the day. The cave had been their home since he was seven. He curled up on the mat beside Mari's and went to sleep.

The next morning, he dressed in the only clothes he owned —ragged pants and a stained shirt along with his worn-out sandals. Mari's dress was short and tattered and her sandals no longer fit. Soon he would be able to buy her some clothes.

After gathering wood for the fire pit, he showed her how to use her energy to make a spark. Several tries later, Mari succeeded.

"Can I make the fire when I get home?" she asked excitedly.

"I'll help you gather more wood so you'll have enough."

Their home was at the base of Dos Santos Mountains, hidden in the forest where there were plenty of dead branches to gather. The main trail through Denoy led to the next village, but the trail to their cave was concealed by trees and thick underbrush. He placed the kindling they gathered against the far wall of the cave.

He walked with Mari to the Academy through the woods as usual. He heard the birds chirping and small animals scurrying under brush. Denoy was set in a clearing, surrounded by the forest on three sides and the mountains on the other. Vaedra, their sun, was bright and warm as always in a cloudless sky. The homes were all dome-shaped brownish-red dwellings clustered on either side of a dirt road in the center. The road led from the forest and ended at the shipyards near the Academy. One of those homes used to be theirs.

He had to beg the Headmaster to let him bring Mari to class with him when she was an infant. He explained to Torres their only aunt lived in Eloy, another village on Tarsius. He hadn't seen her since before his mother died and didn't know how to contact her.

It took a while for Mari to adjust but the instructors had given him plenty of latitude when they learned his mother had died and his father disappeared on the same day. Eventually, the instructors got used to having Mari around.

The day dragged on. His studies held no interest for him. All he thought about was the chance for a better life and learning some new skills. Finally, the alarm sounded and the classes dispersed. He spotted Mari, heading down the steps of the brownish-red colored building. He hurried to her.

"Mari!"

She turned at the sound of her name.

"Go straight home and stay in the back of the cave, Mari."

"I will. When will you come home?"

"I'll be there before dark. You can start the fire just before then." Their lives would be different after today. Maybe soon they would have a dwelling to call home, instead of a cave.

He squatted down and hugged her. "I'll be home as soon as I can. I love you, Mari."

"I love you, too, Berto."

He raced to the area that once housed a thriving ship-building business. Some time ago, something happened that caused them to stop production. Ignacio's Repair Shop was just before the gated entrance to the Denoy Ship Yards.

"You must be Berto," a short, round man said. Ignacio's tan was darker than his own.

"Yes, sir. Headmaster Torres sent me."

"Come, let me show you my shop." Ignacio pointed out the sections of the shop where certain work was performed. There were women and boys, slightly older than himself, working in all the areas. The first was the navigation section, then a thruster section. Another section was devoted to cooling and heating, another for life support systems, and the main section was for engine systems.

"Since production was halted at the shipyards, I've been busy repairing all the old ships. I'll start you off with the thruster section. I expect you to be here every day until dark. You get paid once a week. Do you have a place to stay?"

"For tonight, sir."

"There's Community housing over there." He pointed to a tall, dome-shaped light brown building across the way. "They serve two meals a day. Do you have any questions?"

"Uh, yes sir. I have a younger sister that I'm responsible for. I was wondering if I could...well...bring her to work with me? I promise she won't be any trouble. She's quiet and she'll study while I work."

Ignacio studied him. "What about your parents?"

"It's just me and Mari."

"How have you survived?"

"I'd rather not say, sir, but we've managed. I really need this job."

"You hiding something, boy. Doing anything...illegal?"

"No sir. It's just...I don't want to leave Mari alone. She's too young."

"Torres said you were a hard worker. I'm willing to give you a chance. All right, be here after classes tomorrow—both of you. Maybe I can find something for her to do as well."

"Yes, sir! You won't regret this. Thank you, sir." He shook hands with Ignacio and hurried out the door.

Berto ran as fast as he could through the village to the path in the woods that led to the cave they called home. As he approached the rocky cliffs, he thought he heard muffled sounds. When he got to the mouth of the cave, darkness had settled over the forest.

A piercing scream cut through his heart. Mari!

The dim glow from the fire showed three shadowy figures about his size, leaning over something...Mari!

Oh God! One held her arms down, another held her legs. A third person was on top of her, trying to rape her. The boy's white-blond hair and blue eyes marked him as Chromian.

"No!" Berto's shout echoed throughout the cave as his anger and adrenalin surged through his body, his gut tightening. He lunged for the boy on top, but the energy built up inside him shot out through his hands before he reached him, throwing the boy across the cave, slamming his head against the wall.

As his rage built, his adrenalin pumped faster throughout his body. He reached for the boy holding down Mari's arms, the energy surged again, throwing the boy against another wall. The boy hit the rock hard then slumped over.

He glared at the last boy, who held Mari's legs, moving toward him. He fisted his hands at his sides to keep from doing more harm, but the boy ran out of the cave. The last boy and the second one, with their brown skin and eyes, were Tarsian, like himself and Mari, but he didn't recognize either of them.

He scooped up Mari and hugged her tight. She clung to him, weeping. His heart pounded from the ordeal. His mind was dizzy with comprehension of his newly discovered skill. He had only pulled things toward himself or started fires with his power but this was new. He could feel Mari's body trembling...or was that him?

"Mari, I promise, I will never leave you alone again."

They were no longer safe here. He helped her dress, gathered the few belongings they had, and left the cave, carrying her in his arms.

2

———

Tinnian Space Port, Planet Chroma, 14 anos (years) later

"Give it up, Shey. You're wasting your time," her father, Kaal, said.

"Searching for my brother's killer is wasting my time? How can you say that?" Shey responded.

"Kalen was a bad seed, like my brother. I tried, Shey. I gave him more chances than he deserved. Drop this search. If the Tarsian police had any leads, they would have found the killer fourteen anos ago."

"My involvement with the I.S.P. will give me access to their databases. I will find his killer, Kaal, one way or another." She put her hands on her hips. Whether Kaal liked it or not.

"Then what, Shey? What will you do?"

"I'll make sure that justice is served." Or the killer is dead.

"Will you? What if you find Kalen deserved his fate?"

"What do you mean?" Her heart skipped a beat.

"Check all the facts, Shey, before someone else's life is ruined."

She nodded and Kaal hugged her. How could Kalen deserve to be killed?

"I love you, Shey. You're all I've got. I wish you'd reconsider and work for me. I could use a good pilot like you."

Shey lowered her gaze. She wanted revenge for her brother's death.

"Live your life. Don't waste it searching for Kalen's killer."

"I'll contact you when I can." She kissed her father's cheek. Slinging the duffle over her shoulder, she headed for Docking Bay Two.

The place was deserted at 0400 hours, Chromian time. Her steps echoed through the massive dwelling. She could easily pilot a small craft and fly to Tarsius herself, but she would have to abandon the ship for the duration of her training. Not worth it.

Her piloting skills and teaching background got her into the I.S.P., but it was her chance to find her brother's killer that spurred her on. Her father's words played over in her mind.

Thirty minutes later, the security checks finished, the commercial ship was on its way to Tarsius.

The spacious hall ways and and rich appointments throughout the ship were overwhelming to her. She was not used to such luxury, but since the Interplanetary Space Patrol paid for her trip, she couldn't refuse.

She found her cabin on the lower deck. Tossing the heavy duffle on the floor, she plopped down on the richly covered, velvety bed, resting her head against the soft pillows. This was a new beginning for her and she looked forward to it.

Two days later, the cruiser pulled up to Docking Bay Five at the Quinna Space Port on Tarsius. A large holo flashed "I.S.P. Space Recruits Here." This space port was crowded with various races of people. Chromians from her planet, Tarsians, Persians, Atrians, Vestrians, Plexians, and even Caucus people. Shey headed for the holo and the small group of people gathered there.

While she was a recruit, she would also be the fitness instructor. It meant a lot of time studying for her officer's test, as well as learning everything else the recruits had to learn, but she was up for it. After all, she had sailed through the teaching Academy on Chroma and learned to pilot cargo ships at a much younger age.

"Good afternoon everyone, I'm Flight Instructor Bover. Follow me to Docking Bay Seven." The Atrian, with his darker skin and short-cropped, blue-black hair, turned and headed toward Bay Seven with the small group in tow.

Besides herself, there was one other woman among them. A petite Tarsian woman of maybe five and half centikiks glanced up at her. Her short, spiky black hair with red tips reminded her of a fire stick.

"Are you a space recruit as well?" the fire stick asked.

"You could say that."

"Well, at least I'm not the only woman."

She looked tougher than some of the taller men who followed Bover. An assortment of Tarsian, Chromian, Atrian, and Vestrian men ensued. This would be an interesting trip if nothing else.

They reached the I.S.P. cruiser docked at Bay Seven.

Next to Bover stood a Chromian with a comm-pad. He called out names and rooming assignments. The commercial liner she'd arrived on dwarfed the I.S.P. cruiser. Hopefully, the ride would be decent since Meta was a three-day trip.

"Tam and Shey," the Chromian called out.

"Yo!" the fire stick replied.

Shey raised her hand.

"You two are on deck three, cabin three."

"Thank you, sir," Shey said. The Chromian handed each of them a yav.

"FI Bover will hold orientation in the eating hall in ten minutes. Welcome aboard."

Meta Station, Meta, a moon of Plexus, 3 days later

Berto hadn't seen Mari in four anos. She was only seventeen when he was forced to work for Dram. He had given her the money he received from the pirates to find their aunt and take care of herself. He would ask Howell if he could look for Mari after completing their first mission.

He carried a stack of towels to the fitness room. He heard rumors of Shey's return. There was only one reason she would come back to Meta Station. Revenge. He had looked forward to some time off before her ship arrived but when he saw it hovering over the landing pad, his pulse kicked up a notch. As he rounded the corner, Law Enforcement Officer Danner hurried toward him in the hall, a comm-pad in hand.

"Just think, Berto, after today, no more grunt work. You'll be a full-fledged recruit."

"You mean it gets better?" Being a recruit was a step up

in life. From now on, he would be working with the law instead of against it.

Danner shrugged. "It depends on how fast you learn. Lander has your comm-pad with the rooming list at communications."

Berto nodded as he opened the fitness room with his yav, while Danner disappeared around the corner for final room inspection. Calling them officers felt strange. When he first met the men stationed here, they were all agents of the I.S.P. With Dram's capture, the new program was born along with everyone's promotion.

Berto set the towels on a shelf against the far wall in an otherwise empty room. Dram's old room. Except for the new yellow coloring on the walls, the renovations hadn't changed much of the look to the old slave trading compound. It would take time getting used to calling the place the Interplanetary Space Patrol, Meta Station.

He rubbed the back of his neck where the implant was located. He'd almost forgotten about it. A little gift from the pirates who paid him to steal the cargo ship that Dram stole from him. Well, after four anos, he should be safe by now.

He locked up. Pointless, he thought, since the equipment hadn't arrived, but Lander gave him the order to do it. He headed toward communications.

"There you are," Lander turned toward him as the door hissed open. Lander stood tall and stocky behind Communications Officer Derek, while Derek worked the Comm-board's frequency module.

"Here." Lander handed him the comm-pad.

Berto powered up the device and anxiously scrolled for

the names of the new recruits. More than halfway down the list, her name caught his eye and gave his heart a hitch. Shey.

"Have you got all the rooms prepped?" Lander asked, pulling him from his memories of her.

"Everything is good to go." He cleared his throat.

"The ship just landed. After Danner greets them, you can show the recruits to their rooms."

Danner hurried into the room through the double doors.

"Ready, boys?" Danner glanced at both of them.

He wasn't ready for Shey, that's for sure, but she had been on his mind since the day they'd met, over two Meta-moon cycles ago.

The three of them stepped outside. The hatch lowered on the class C cargo transport and he held his breath as the first recruits stepped off the ship.

Shey stepped out on the ramp behind some of the taller men, glancing around her former prison. She repressed the feelings she had the first time she arrived here against her will.

"Welcome to Meta Station. I'm Procurement Officer Lander and this is Law Enforcement Officer Danner."

She moved to her right to see who spoke and her breath caught in her throat at the sight of Berto. What was he doing here? The sight of him excited her. Then anger merged with it at the thought of her past abduction.

"Meta is the second I.S.P. training facility in the Vaedra System," LEO Danner began. "You are all part of a special-missions team set up to locate and retrieve slaves who have been abducted from their home planets by the slave trader,

Dram. This six-week program is geared to get you in shape and prepare you mentally and physically for the demands of the job." LEO Danner paced before them as he spoke.

"After our evening meal, we will have a tour of Meta, then a small social gathering before calling it a night."

He turned, gesturing toward her former abductor. "This is Berto. He'll escort you to your quarters and later give you the Meta tour."

How can a criminal work for the I.S.P.? Unless they didn't know he was a criminal.

"Follow me," Berto said. He cleared his throat as he walked through the outer door and into the communications room.

She would get to the bottom of this. Of all the people working on the mission, how could they let a man with a criminal past be a part of this? Her heart pounded at the thought of confronting him.

"This is Communications Officer Derek. He'll give each of you a frequency ID so you can send and receive communications off Meta."

Berto either deliberately ignored her or he didn't recognize her. Maybe she read more into their brief encounters.

"I'll have them ready by morning meal. You can check with me then," CO Derek said.

Berto lead them through the double doors into the eating hall.

"As you can see, this is where we'll spend some quality time, depending on the skills of the new cook." He glanced at the group and caught her gaze. "You did bring a cook with you, didn't you?"

Her heartbeat kicked up a notch when she realized he spoke to her. "He's with the officers," she replied, crossing her arms over her chest. He recognized her.

"At least we won't starve." He led the group through another set of double doors.

He pointed to the lounge area to the left. "This is our waiting area and beside it, Commander Howell's office. Through the office, our only classroom. We'll get to know each other well by the end of the training program." He caught her gaze once more, a warm sensation running through her. What did he imply?

Continuing down the hall, he pointed to the rooms on the right. "These are the officer's quarters. On the left, we have the fitness room and the female quarters." At the T intersection of halls, Berto pointed to the four rooms and called out "Crocker, Dayton, Tibu and Kar. Your quarters, room one." He pointed to the last door. Then he called out "Zed, Meffa, Talo and Grimm. Your quarters, room two." He pointed to the second room from the left. Then he called "Coz, Sags, Telik. Room three. I'll call for you all when it's time for the evening meal."

The group of men headed for their quarters as Berto turned toward her and Tam. Her pulse raced in anticipation.

"Tam, these are your quarters," he pointed to the last room on the left before the intersection of halls.

"I have my own room?"

"Apparently," he checked his comm-pad again.

Tam shrugged and entered her quarters through the hissing door.

Shey had to let Commander Howell know about Berto's past. He could jeopardize the missions.

Berto locked gazes with her. "Why are you here?"

"I could ask you the same thing. I want to speak with Commander Howell."

He turned, leading her to Howell's office in silence. He

hesitated by the door panel. She didn't have time for this. She pushed past him, the door hissed open.

Howell sat at his desk, working from his processor when he glanced up.

"What is he doing here?" She pointed to Berto, throwing her duffle to the ground. Crossing her arms, she glared at Commander Howell. She recognized him as one of the men in charge of the rescue efforts on Vestra Minor and the one who recruited her. Certainly he knew about Berto's past. Her heart pounded in her chest.

"Berto is a reformed criminal, Shey," Howell began. "He is stationed here, along with everyone else, until training is over. Afterward, he will be on missions just like you and the others, searching for the slaves that Dram traded over the years."

"How can you let him work here after what he'd done?" she demanded.

"He's confessed his crimes and this is his punishment."

"Punishment?" What kind of punishment was that? He should be serving time on Plumaris like other criminals.

"Can I speak, sir?" Berto asked.

"Go ahead, Berto." Howell rested his elbows beside his processor, propping up his chin with his knuckles.

"Yes, go ahead. I'd like to know what makes you think you can be an I.S.P. agent after living a life of crime." She shoved her hands on her hips. Abducting women and children was about as low as one could get.

"Look, I did what I had to in the past to survive, but I don't expect you to understand that. My sister depended on me. Working for Dram was not my idea. I was blackmailed into it. Now it's over."

Blackmailed?

"I co-operated with the I.S.P. to capture him and a few of

his employees. I volunteered to help locate all those he had sold into slavery until everyone is found, in return for my freedom."

Freedom? What about all those abducted? What about their freedom?

"I expect to be here for as long as it takes. If that means for life, then so be it." He turned toward Commander Howell. "And after our first mission, if it's all right with you, sir, I'd like to locate my sister to make sure she's taken care of."

He has a sister that he cares about. She remembered her brother and how he spent time with her when he was alive. "That doesn't excuse what you did to me and the others."

"No, it doesn't. I don't expect you to forgive me. All I can say is...I'm sorry." He held her gaze. "I'm really sorry, for everything."

His dark brown eyes held a deep sadness she couldn't overlook. Maybe he meant it.

Howell cleared his throat. "Everyone makes mistakes, Shey. I also think that people deserve a second chance. Now, can we get back to the business at hand?"

"Yes, sir," Berto said, stepping back.

She studied him before crossing her arms again, her opinion of him softening. Never had a man apologized to her before.

"Berto will show you and the others to your quarters," Howell glanced at his chrono, "if he hasn't already done that. Later, he'll give the group a tour of the grounds since he knows this place better than anyone. Tomorrow, he is a recruit like everyone else. I expect you to treat him like you would all the others. Is that clear?"

She swallowed. "Yes sir." She grabbed her duffle and left. Berto held the door for her. Another kindness.

"Let me show you to your quarters," he said.

"I think I can remember the way, thank you." She trudged down the hall carrying her duffle over her shoulder.

Berto cleared his throat. She turned to glance back at him. "Your quarters," he pointed one door past the fitness room.

"I thought..."

"The old slave quarters are now the rooms for the male recruits. Your quarters are next to the fitness room." He punched in a code on the door panel, then handed her the yav.

She let her gaze slowly roam up his muscular body, covered in the white unicrin of the I.S.P., before resting on his sad, brown eyes. "Thank you." She stepped inside the doorframe and turned to face him. Something about him drew her like a magnet.

He crossed his arms, clutching his comm-pad, the muscles in his arms and shoulders stretching the fabric of his unicrin. She had forgotten how good he looked.

"Why are you really here?" he asked.

Her heart skipped a beat. While she never expected to see him again, she couldn't tell him about her fantasies. She dropped her duffle on the floor, placing her hands on either side of the doorframe. "I have...unfinished business to take care of." She lowered her gaze. After her outburst in Howell's office, Berto wouldn't want to be alone with her. Besides, her revenge was her own business.

"So you quit your instructor's job at the academy and joined the I.S.P.?"

"Not quite." She glanced up and caught his gaze. "They asked me not to come back." She crossed her arms, the memory of that day still painful.

"Oh?" He raised an eyebrow.

"The headmaster said he no longer needed my services." She clenched her jaw and leaned against the doorframe.

"Why? You did all you could to protect those girls."

"That's what I thought." She straightened, uncrossing her arms. "The headmaster said that I should have stopped you from abducting us in the first place." She lowered her gaze and punched the lock tab. The door closed in his face.

She leaned against the wall of her new home and let out a breath, fanning herself. The man still affected her. It was all she could do to keep from touching him.

Berto slowly exhaled. Shey's unfinished business—most likely revenge against him. He couldn't blame her. If she had tried to stop him, like her headmaster suggested, he would have had to kill her. His instructions were to pick up young girls on Chroma. A fitness instructor wasn't part of the plan. But because she intrigued him, she was still alive.

3

______

Shey glanced around her quarters. The massive bed took up the entire room, with the exception of space for a dresser and mirror. The furniture was made of tulin, set against tan-colored walls. The remnants of Dram's slave business, no doubt. Certainly the I.S.P. didn't have that kind of kashis.

She unpacked her things, finding places for her belongings. She would have to see about her fitness equipment. Six weeks wasn't enough time to get everyone into shape.

Her thoughts drifted back to Berto. She knew her hostility toward him was because he abducted her and her students but he wasn't the only one involved in the abduction. Berto had always been kind to them. They were all slaves for a brief period of time. The actual work in the fields didn't hurt them and she was able to make a game of it with the girls to get them to harvest the vegetables. Was she mad at Berto because she lost her job? No, she was more disappointed in the Headmaster. But Berto was Tarsian and she was Chromian, two races who could not mix without being exiled. At least, that was the mandate. All she wanted to do was kiss him, but she couldn't tell him that, and it was forbidden.

Her heart hammered in her chest. Was she mad at herself for wanting a Tarsian man instead of someone of her own race? There was no one on Chroma she was interested in and her time for being chosen as someone's mate had passed. Most mates were chosen at a much younger age than her twenty-eight anos. Besides, instructors weren't allowed to fraternize with the students. She would have plenty of studying to keep her mind off him. At least, she hoped so.

Berto paced beside the pond. No longer having a room to himself, he found this quiet, outside corner of the building a safe haven for thoughts. Getting thoughts of Shey out of his head was difficult with her here. He sorted through his shock of seeing her just by taking in the serenity of this place.

His friend, Adam of Earth, once told him that this spot had reminded him of his home back in Tennessee. He couldn't believe Adam had been determined to leave Genesis once they found her father. He tried to talk Adam into staying because the two of them were destined to be mates. He saw it in their eyes when they looked at each other. He wanted what they had, but with his past life of crime, he didn't deserve that kind of happiness. He wondered if Adam had changed his mind. He glanced at his chrono, then headed inside. He went to Shey's quarters first, pressing the buzzer panel on her door.

"Yes?" Shey called from inside.

"It's Berto. I've come to escort you to the facilities tour."

The door hissed open. All rational thoughts escaped at

the sight of her in that soft pink tunic, covering matching pants that hid her shoes. Her face glowed with the freshness of the new equinox. The color suited her well. He licked his dry lips at the thought of tasting her.

"I've come to—"

Shey glanced past him. "Where are the others?"

"I started with you this time," he said, trying to quiet his racing heart.

"Well, I'm impressed," she said, holding his gaze while joining him in the hall. A smile escaped his lips, but his mind went blank as her gaze deepened.

"And where are we going?" she asked. The sight of her pale blue eyes penetrated his thoughts.

He shook the fuzziness from his brain and pointed to Tam's quarters. He pressed the buzzer panel. Too late to have a private conversation with Shey. He clenched his teeth. Damn, she looked good.

Tam's door hissed open. She glanced at Shey, then him, then out in the hall. Tam had changed into a black tunic and pants.

"We must be the privileged few," Tam said.

"Well, we can't always be last, now, can we?" Shey said, crossing her arms.

The two women flanked him on either side as they walked toward the intersection of halls.

He buzzed room one. "Time for your afternoon tour," he announced. The men filed out into the hall. All of them had changed clothes. Room two emptied out, then his room. He felt self conscious in his unicrin. The others had worn unicrins when they arrived.

"I've shown you most of the facilities already," he began, "except for the important parts." He led them to the end of the hall and stopped in front of a set of double hissing doors.

Inside, two large cleaning machines and two large moisture evaporators sat against the wall, separated by a long table with two chairs.

"We're responsible for our own laundry at Meta Station. You can access these machines any time, but don't leave them unattended with your clothes in them or Officer Lander will confiscate your garments. There's no telling what he'll make you do to get them back." He remembered his own first experience with the man. His payback was moving furniture and re-arranging sleeping quarters.

He demonstrated how to operate the machines and pointed out where the cleaning chemicals were stored. "You are responsible for your own quarters. Officer Lander will inspect them once a week, so keep them clean. He likes to inflict pain when all his hard work has been thwarted."

"Did I hear someone mention my name?" Lander said, coming toward them in his unicrin. Relief ran through Berto. The man stood a head taller than the tallest recruit, dwarfing Tam. All faces turned toward Lander.

"I explained that you would inspect their quarters weekly," he said.

"Yes and there will be penalties for messy rooms. Did you show them how to use the laundry system?" Lander asked.

"We're just finishing up," he said. He knew Lander didn't tolerate sloppiness.

"Carry on." Lander glanced at his chrono. "I'll see all of you in the eating hall." He turned and left the group.

"At the opposite end of this hall," Berto continued, "you see two doors. One is an exterior door, the other, the supply room."

Everyone turned to look. "You'll find all the supplies you'll need to keep your quarters clean. You can access that room at any time as well."

He led them back to the main hall, stopping outside the fitness room.

"Our fitness room." He opened the door with his yav, and showed the empty room to the group. Shey stepped around him, glancing inside.

"Hmmm, seems the equipment isn't here yet," she said.

"I believe it came in on the cargo ship," he said, swallowing hard at her nearness.

Shey glared at him, holding his gaze. "I suggest you get it in this room so we can use it in the morning."

He let out a breath after she moved into the hallway. He glanced up. *Why me?*

Moving down the hall, he led the group to the lounge then the training room. The chairs faced a long desk with a large holo-vid screen behind it. At the desk were four flight simulators. "This is the classroom we will use most of the time." He turned, leading everyone into the eating hall.

Once inside, he pointed to the door to the left of the room. "That's the food prep room."

The door opened. A burly-looking man pushed a large cart with several containers of steaming food into the room.

"Food prep is off limits to all of you," the burly man announced. "If you're late for a meal, you go hungry." He placed the cart against the left wall beside a small cabinet.

"Clean plates and utensils," he pointed to the cabinet. "Dirty plates and utensils," he pointed to a bucket under the cart of food containers. "Any questions?" He dared anyone to speak with his angry gaze. Turning, he exited through the food prep entry.

"When will we go on the tour of Meta?" Shey asked, standing a little too close.

His pulse raced at her nearness. "After our evening meal." He'd rather give her a private tour of Meta. Yeah, like that would ever happen.

"Instructors sit here." Berto gestured to the nearest table. "All others sit over there." He gestured to the two farthest tables.

The group of men, Tam, and Shey gathered at the cart, selecting their food. The other instructors and staff filed in, lining up at the cart as the rest found places at the tables.

Shey sat at the instructors' table. He stopped beside her seat and leaned down, whispering in her ear.

"You're in the wrong section, Shey."

"No, I'm not."

"The recruits sit over there." He pointed to the other tables.

"I'm your new physical fitness instructor."

His mouth dropped open, his throat dry. He was so kunnarled. "My mistake. I thought you were...a recruit."

He backed away, joining his quarters-mates at the table. His heart sank like a stone in the pond. Shey was off limits. He was a recruit, a neophyte, and must undergo the same requirements as the other recruits. He just hoped he could handle the revenge she would dish out toward him.

Digging into his trew, a bowl of vegetables with meat and a thick gravy, he relished the taste, realizing he had worked up an appetite. Could he get through this day without further incident? He put off thinking about what would happen later, while the most beautiful woman he had ever seen was now his PT instructor. He imagined her the way he saw her the last time she was here, wearing a short, yellow shim with her thick blonde hair pulled back into a braid. And those long legs of hers, mmmm.

"How long have you been here, Berto?" Telik asked.

He thought back to his first encounter with this place, a feeling of apprehension about what he'd gotten himself into.

"Four anos," he replied.

"You've been with the I.S.P. four anos and you're still a recruit?" Sags asked.

"No. I worked for Dram all that time as a systems tech on cargo ships and smaller class-A wing ships." Stealing, repairing, changing ID codes of those ships as well, but they didn't need to know that. "I'm a new recruit, just like the rest of you," Berto said.

"Who is this...Dram?" Coz asked.

"You'll learn more about him in your training classes, gentlemen," Howell interrupted as he walked near the table. Howell pulled out a seat from the head of the instructors' table. Beside him on either side sat Danner, Shey, Lander and four men he had never seen before.

"Welcome to Meta, gentlemen, and ladies, I am Commander Howell. To my right, I have Law Enforcement Officer Danner and History and Cultures Officer Semm, along with Cower, our cook. To my left, Physical Training Officer Shey, Flight Instructor Bover, Procurement Officer Lander, and assistant cook Tabon. They will be your instructors throughout this training."

Berto glanced in Shey's direction, her back toward him.

"Tonight, we'll have a small social gathering in the gardens at 2000 hours. After dinner, you will have a tour of Meta on board the Galatin. Tomorrow will begin with the PT class at 0600 hours, outside the comm-room. The morning meal will follow at 0700 hours. Enjoy your meal."

Howell sat down, continuing a private conversation with his officers.

Coz leaned close to Berto. "I wouldn't mind getting to know Shey a little better," he whispered.

His stomach hardened at Coz's words. "She's off limits," he said, clenching his teeth.

"Why, because we're recruits?" Coz asked.

No, because I saw her first, tozat brain. "Something like that," he said. He looked down at his trew, avoiding Coz's glance.

"You know the mandate, Coz," Telik whispered. "No one can take a mate from another race."

Shey was Chromian. He had abducted her and the twenty-nine students she taught that fateful day from Chroma, an incident etched in his memory forever. The four of them sitting at the table were Tarsian and they could take only Tarsian mates.

"The Council of Nations would have to find out before you would be exiled," Sags said, stirring his trew. "I'm sure they have more important things to work on than locating people who take mates from other races."

"How could they enforce such a mandate, anyway?" Coz asked.

"Besides, Dram's slave trading business pretty much destroyed that mandate," Sags added.

"How do you mean?" Coz asked.

"The slaves were taken to different planets, for labor." He took a bite of his trew.

"That wasn't the only reason," Telik suggested.

Berto knew the truth of it. He had seen it happen. Many of the slave women were used as mates in remote areas. The men, for labor. Shey's group was used for farming. Thank

God, his friend Adam had talked him into rescuing Shey and her students.

"I think it's time we changed all that," Sags whispered.

"How do you plan to do that?" Coz asked.

"Elections are coming up," Telik said.

"Yes. Contor is running from Efla in the Eloy Sector of Tarsius. He has made it clear that we should decide ourselves what mate we want, and not let the mandate choose for us," Sags said.

"I agree," Berto said, tearing his bread. "I know before the Exodus, Vestra Major wanted to preserve the races for future generations. But let's admit it, some women from other races are...more appealing...than Tarsian women," he said, low enough Tam would not overhear him. The thought of holding Shey's warm body against his flashed through his mind. "Besides, what Dram did cannot be undone, whether anyone likes it or not."

"What sector are you from?" Sags asked.

"Denoy."

"Isn't that the sector where the great Shaman, Incanta, lived?" Telik asked.

He shrugged, hoping the men would lose interest in the subject.

"Yes, she lived there and was reported to have some tele-kinetic powers," Sags continued.

"I've heard of her, too," Coz said, finishing off his trew. "She had two children whose powers were greater than hers."

"I heard that she could control the elements just by willing it," Telik added.

Berto shook his head. "I never heard those stories." Of course his mother never mentioned them. Some of those things happened before his birth. He knew her seven anos, and had seen her do such things before she died. He shared her gift, using his for survival.

Mari had the gift as well, but she used hers sparingly.

"Your parents never told you the stories of Incanta?" Telik asked.

"My mother died when I was young. My father abandoned us the same day." His throat tightened at the buried memory.

Danner stood up at the officer's table. "We'll begin the tour of Meta in about ten minutes," he announced. "Meet outside the communications entrance."

Ten minutes later, eighteen people stood outside the comm-room doorway.

"Gentlemen and ladies, would you mind stepping aboard the Galatin? We'll begin our tour of Meta in a few minutes," Danner said.

Danner patted him hard on the back as they walked up the steep ramp together. Thoughts of escape crossed his mind as his chest tightened.

The Galatin, an elongated shuttle with viewing screens up and down either side, sat on the landing pad. The cockpit's viewing screen took up the entire front of the shuttle, with a smaller screen on either side. The body of the ship was separated from the cockpit by an opaque wall with an opening in the middle.

The cockpit held four seats. He made the fifth person. He knelt down between the two front seats, his pulse kicking up a notch at Shey's closeness. Danner piloted on the left, while Shey sat on his right. Bover and Semm sat behind him.

"I'll flip on the comm switch so you can describe the scenery," Danner said.

Danner lifted the Galatin up about three centikiks, taking off in the direction of the valley.

Berto spoke about the wildlife and described the valley as briefly as possible, savoring Shey's nearness. Beyond the valley, the ground sloped up to the tall cliffs where vegetation covered more of the area. "This is the Rift Mountain range, which encircles Meta. The wildlife found here are eeya, temits, and kabors. The eeya are shy creatures that feed off the sparse vegetation. The temits fly around seeking grice that wander this far, as well as sprats. The kabors feed off of eeya, and any unsuspecting person who looks tasty," he said, glancing at Shey, licking his lips.

Shey narrowed her brows at him.

Danner took them into the mountains to three great ponds, surrounded by lush, green vegetation.

"Are there any pesca in the ponds?" Semm asked.

"Yes, but I've never had the opportunity to catch any," he said.

Past the ponds, they came upon another valley, similar to Mira. "This is the Nica Valley," Berto said. "The same wildlife in Mira is found here. On occasion, though, a kabor wanders through here since the Rift Mountains are closer to this side."

Past the Nica, Danner brought the Galatin back to the compound.

"Why is there more vegetation here at the compound?" Bover asked.

"Dram brought these plants and trees from Earth because it reminded him of the place where he stayed until his rescue by a salvage ship," he said.

Danner set the Galatin down on a landing pad beside the compound, flipping off the comm switch.

"Thanks, Berto," Danner said, rising from his seat.

"I can't wait to learn more about this...Dram," Semm said. "He sounds interesting."

"Interesting is the nicest thing you could say about the man," Berto said.

Shey glared at him. "How can you say that?" Anger welled up in her face as she stood, her arms crossed.

"I said it was the nicest. I can think of many unpleasant ways to describe him," Berto said, fighting the urge to touch her.

The others filed off the ship. He waited his turn as Shey stood close. He swallowed, facing her. "If it's any consolation, Shey, I'd do anything to make amends for the hurt I've caused you."

She raised a brow. "Anything?"

He nodded, mesmerized by her pale blue eyes. His throat went dry.

"Meet me outside the comm-room in a few minutes," she said.

His gut told him he would regret this.

4

This was her chance for sweet revenge. But how could she get him alone? Even if she could corner him in her room, everyone would notice they were missing.

She stepped into the comm-room where PO Lander and CO Derek were discussing something.

"Excuse me, sirs, but do either of you know if my fitness equipment has been set up?"

"The equipment is still in the crates outside, PT Officer Shey. Do you need help setting it up?" PO Lander asked.

"I've got help, thank you." She turned and went back outside.

Now if she could pull this off...

Berto headed across the outside compound for the comm-room.

"That was an impressive tour tonight," Shey said, coming from behind him.

He turned at the sound of her voice. "Uh, thanks." He crossed his arms over his chest, trying to slow his racing heart. "What is it you want, PT Officer Shey?" Not only curious but skeptical from his gut warning. He also had to remember she was an officer who had every reason to hate him and no reason to forgive him for abducting her.

"You know I have all this equipment here." She nodded toward the crates.

He clenched his teeth, bracing himself for what would come next.

Shey moved close. "I need someone," she began as she dragged a finger across his chest to his shoulder, "to help me with all this fitness equipment." She moved behind him, dragging her finger across his back and other shoulder.

His pulse quickened as his flesh reacted to her touch. Anticipation built inside him.

"And you waited until dark to ask for help?" he asked.

"You know I need this for class tomorrow," her voice pleaded with him.

"We have a social in thirty minutes," he said, glancing at his chrono. "Your absence will be noticed." He was puzzled at her request.

"Oh, I'm planning on being there. You're the one who won't be." She turned and left.

His mouth fell open and his heart sank. Then anger and hurt tore at him. This social would have been the closest he had ever been to a party in his life. He clenched his fists.

"If that's the way she wants to play, so be it."

Shey paced the floor of her quarters. She came close to overlooking the fact that Berto had abducted her and her students from Chroma. After all, he participated in their rescue. If it hadn't been for that fact, she would never forgive him. He had worked for Dram for over four anos, though, and that was a criminal act she had difficulty dealing with.

She glanced at her chrono. If she spent an hour at the social, that should give Berto time to set up some of the equipment. She would join him then to help him finish the job. This would certainly be an interesting evening since there were only two females on this entire moon.

She hurriedly dressed and left for the social. Yes, she wanted revenge. She was entitled to it after what happened. But the revenge she longed for was for him to hold her and kiss her with those full, tempting lips. Then she wanted her way with him, all of him, to do as she pleased.

Berto yanked the fasteners off the crates with a prytor.

He allowed his anger to funnel through the tool, rather than use his powers destructively. He had to calm down. One at a time, he opened all the crates without obliterating them in the process.

He moved the equipment with a hover-trol to the loading door next to the storage room in the second hall and watched the others head down the main hall to the social outside.

He clenched his teeth, thinking of all those men spending time with Shey. He shook the thoughts from his head and took deep, calming breaths.

Once everything was in the room, he set up the instruction holo.

The ratchet tool he needed was on the far side of the room. He reached his hand out and the tool flew into his opened palm as Tam stepped through the hissing door. Her eyes flashed.

Damn, he should have locked the door.

She wore a floor-length black dress, cut low in the front. She was stunning, with her black, spiked hair with orange-red tips, but something about her just didn't feel right.

"That's an interesting talent you've got there." she said, crossing her arms.

"It comes in handy sometimes." He tried to focus on his work.

Tam moved closer. "I suppose you inherited that skill?"

"What if I did?" He turned to glance at her.

"There is a legend on Tarsius—"

"What is it you want, Tam?" He had to stop her questioning.

"I wanted to see if you were going to the social."

"I'm busy putting together our fitness equipment."

Tam fidgeted with her hands. "Well, I guess I'll just go, then."

He turned back to his work, but sensed her hesitation.

"If you change your mind, I'll save a dance for you."

He glanced back at her. No one ever wanted to dance with him before. "Uh, thanks."

Tam slipped out the door. With a flick of the wrist, he locked the door from across the room.

Following the holo's direction, he attached the pieces of weight lifting equipment. Drawing his powers from within, he pulled the pieces together and held them in place with his mind, while attaching the bolts and fasteners with the ratchet.

Tam's words played over in his mind. The others would be dancing with Shey, holding her tight, whispering in her ear. His arm muscles tightened as he fisted his hands. She wasn't his. His jaw hurt from clenching his teeth so hard. He stood and took a deep breath. He had to stop thinking like that.

He moved on to the running platform. There were more pieces to locate and assemble than he realized. Shey had equipment for strength, agility, flexibility, and cardio. By the time he finished assembling everything, he decided to give himself a workout, following the holo's fitness program. This should keep his mind off Shey.

Satisfied the equipment operated correctly, he packed up the tools and programmed the door to lock. Exhausted and drenched in sweat, he headed to his room.

"Thank you, Commander," Shey said. "If you'll excuse me, I have an early class in the morning." Exhilarated by all the dancing and attention she had gotten, she left the pond area and headed inside. She glanced at her chrono. Guilt slammed into her as she realized how much time had gone by. She had meant to check on Berto after an hour, but it had been more than four hours since she had seen him. A missed opportunity again.

As she approached the fitness room, the door hissed opened.

No one was inside but all the equipment had been set up. She was impressed by the way it was arranged, with plenty of room between the equipment to move around. She would have to thank Berto in the morning. A smile escaped her lips at the thought of him.

~

By the time Berto's head hit the pillow, he was out. It seemed like minutes later when he heard someone's alarm go off.

Telik growled. "Tell me it's still night and that was my imagination."

An illuminator went on and he pulled the covers over his head.

"Hey Berto, when did you get back?"

He sat up and scrubbed his face. "It feels like I just did."

"Where were you last night?" Sags asked. "That was a great social. Shey and Tam danced with everyone."

"Danced?" He stood up, his heart racing. She couldn't wait to get away from him last night. Maybe that was why. "I was setting up our fitness equipment."

"I thought you were going with us to the social," Coz said.

"So did I." He clenched his teeth several times before heading to the cleansing compartment to throw some cold water on his face. He had to wake up. His body was screaming 'sleep', but he had to report to PT in a few minutes.

The four of them headed to the field just beyond the communications door, dressed in their workout clothes. The others joined them.

Shey was there, fresh and beautiful as ever. After lining everyone up, she went over some warming exercises. They practiced the form, while she checked each of them. She stood inches away, her gaze caressing his body. He locked gazes with her and suppressed a smile. Her kiskis fragrance helped calm him, but the pink shorts and loose shirt she wore awakened a need in him. His pulse quickened. He realized he hadn't seen a woman's bare legs since...he worked for Dram. And they had been her legs. He fought the urge to stare.

Slowly, Shey moved around the group, checking everyone while calling out exercises. A few stolen glances convinced him she was still curious. Twenty minutes later, she had everyone running three miles around the valley and back.

He struggled to keep up, his body demanding him to stop, but he pushed himself. Each step felt like craggin weights holding him down. He stumbled forward, and someone caught him on either side. Coz and Sags.

"Keep going, we got you," Coz said.

"I'm slowing you down," he argued.

"We'll help you keep the pace," Sags said.

The three of them were the last to finish. Shey stood at the end, arms crossed over her chest.

"Unacceptable," she said. "You three can run another three miles, on your own." She turned to leave.

"What?" Coz called out. "Berto's exhausted from putting your equipment together all night."

"You, sir, can run six miles," Shey pointed at Coz, then left.

The three of them glanced at each other, mouths open. He had half expected that after the way she treated him last night. She was getting her revenge. Forgiveness was out of the question now.

"That's not the woman I danced with last night," Coz said.

Sags shook his head. "Come on, let's get this over with so we can eat. I'm getting hungry."

The pain in his chest was not from the run, but from the hurt he felt from her stinging words. Did she know about his past? He hadn't told anyone about that except Captain Luc, and his friend Adam. If treating him like yuka dung was her idea of revenge, then he could take it since he messed up her life when he abducted her. "I'm sorry men. I didn't mean to get you two in trouble."

"Hey, we're in this together," Sags said.

"At least she didn't say how fast we had to run," Coz said.

The other two trotted off ahead, while he kept a steady pace. He forced what energy he had left to keep himself from falling down.

By the time he finished his second three-mile run, Coz had finished his extra six miles, and they headed into the eating hall. The door hissed open at their approach.

No one inside. He checked his chrono, 0830 hours. He walked into the food prep room, Coz followed.

Tabon looked up from wiping the counter. "You missed the morning meal."

"Got anything left?" Coz asked.

"Maybe." Tabon opened the food restorer and pulled out a small tray. "I figured some of you would miss the first meal." He set the tray before them and pulled out a couple of eating implements. "Help yourselves."

"Did Sags get anything to eat?" he asked.

"No one else came through here after 0800," Tabon said.

"I'll bring him something," he said. He split the portion into thirds and set some on a plate for Sags. He and Coz split the rest and he wolfed down his share.

"You know classes begin at 0900 hours, right?" Tabon asked.

He looked at his chrono, then at Coz, and grabbed the small plate, while shoveling the last bit into his mouth. He rushed out the door with Coz following close behind.

When they reached their quarters, Sags stepped out of the cleansing compartment. Telik stretched out on the bed.

"For you." He shoved the plate into Sags' hand and rushed into the cleansing area.

There were four compartments. He took one, and Coz took another. While showering, he found himself thinking of Shey and what he really wanted to do with her. If he could move things without touching them, maybe he could touch her...with his mind.

5

———

Semm addressed the class as Berto slipped into an empty seat in the back of the room.

"For those of you who don't know the story, Dram used this base camp for his slave trading operations. He had been in business for nearly twenty-five anos, so the first slaves he traded may not be interested in returning to their home planets."

"Why wouldn't they want to go home?" Tam asked.

"When someone has been gone that long, they tend to adapt to their surroundings and accept their situation, giving up hope of returning home. They may even be sympathetic to their captors."

"Why give up hope?"

"In some cases," Semm explained, "some of the slaves were young children. By now, they may not recall the time before their captivity. Slavery would be all they know." He walked to the holo-vid and tapped it on. An image of the Vaedra system came into view.

"From what we've been able to discern," Semm went on, "Dram took people from Chroma and shipped them to

Vestra Minor, Atria, and Persus. He took people from Tarsius and shipped them to Persus and the moon, Ti."

Berto sat up. Tarsius? He had seen the records himself. He de-coded them for the I.S.P. He didn't remember seeing anyone from the planet Tarsius being sent anywhere, least of all, Ti.

"He took people from Atria and shipped them to Persus as well as Ti."

"Why?" Tam asked.

Tam asked too many questions, but Berto was more interested in how Semm got his information.

"The slaves were used for harvesting crops, mining, and building projects," Semm stopped there.

"And some were used for breeding purposes." His stomach knotted at the memory.

Someone gasped, but all heads turned to face him.

"When were the Tarsians abducted?" he asked.

"How did you know about the breeding programs?" Semm asked.

"I delivered some of the shipments to Persus where they were actively breeding with Atrians. When were the Tarsians abducted?"

"Over twenty-one anos ago," Semm said. "They were taken from the Eloy, Denoy, and Torren sectors. In the Tarsian case, however, men were taken from Eloy and Denoy, while young girls were taken from Torren. In most other cases, both men and young girls were taken."

Berto's heart slammed against his chest. Could it be possible that his father didn't abandon him and his sister, but was abducted? The timing was right. And that was also about the time the ship-building factory ceased operations. His father once worked there.

"Why are you here, then?" Tibu, a Chromian recruit, asked.

"For reparation of my sins," he mumbled. If Tibu knew what it was like to work for Dram, he wouldn't have asked.

He heard tsking sounds as the other recruits turned away from him to face Semm.

"For the remainder of the class, we will discuss the different cultures of the races you will be dealing with." Semm drew their attention to the holo-vid.

When the class broke for PT 2, he was out the door first, running into Commander Howell.

"Berto, I'd like to speak with you in my office."

Damn. He stepped out of the way of the others as they filed past him, sneering and tsking when they saw him.

Finally, Shey stopped in front of him.

"Were we meant for a breeding program?"

"Don't flatter yourself, Shey. The girls were sold to Z as labor. You didn't fit into the equation at all. If it wasn't for me, you would have been dead on Chroma."

Shey's mouth fell open.

Commander Howell stepped inside the small office.

"Excuse us, Shey, Berto and I have a matter to take care of."

"Yes, sir," she stepped through the doorway and into the hall.

"You weren't at the social last night." Howell sat at his desk.

"Sorry sir. I had some work to do."

"I thought you had been looking forward to it."

"Yes sir, I was, but I volunteered to put Shey's fitness equipment together. It took all night."

"You volunteered for that?" Howell picked up his empty mug and studied it.

"Yes sir. Someone had to do it. She needs it today for class."

"I could have arranged for someone to help you." Howell set his mug down.

"Everyone else was busy, sir."

"Shey was at the social, being very...social, as I recall."

Howell moved some things on his desk.

"Sir, how did HCO Semm learn about the Tarsian abductions?"

Howell looked up from his desk. "It was information buried within the files. Semm has been on Dram's case from the beginning. Once you de-coded the files, copies were sent to him to decipher. He found files within files. A few had some strategic information leading back to the beginning of Dram's career.

"Semm studied these files to get locations from which to launch our searches. The first search will take place on Persus. Because of Dram's capture, several of us received promotions. Luc is now Admiral. He's ordered backup teams to assist us as needed when we arrive on Persus." Howell glanced at his chrono. "I guess you're late for PT 2 class?"

"Yes sir. Commander, if what Semm said is true, I believe it's possible my father may have been abducted by Dram, and may be on Persus."

Howell sat up in his chair. "We'll find him, then. After securing Persus, we'll start our searches in chronological order."

When the door to the PT class opened, all eyes were on him.

"The next time you're late for class, there will be extra

work to do." Shey turned back to the student on the inclined board.

He scrubbed his face. He wanted to be anywhere but here right now, but his only alternative was Plumaris for his crimes of participating in slave trading. Life on Plumaris didn't sound good to a male of twenty-eight anos.

He watched as Shey allowed each person to try the equipment while she supervised to make sure they performed properly.

As one recruit pulled up to the bar, the weights on one side crashed to the floor, causing the recruit to tumble off the platform.

"Are you all right?" Shey asked, rushing to his side.

"Yes ma'am."

"What happened?" Telik whispered to Berto.

"I don't know. Everything functioned properly last night when I worked out," he whispered back.

Shey went to each piece of equipment, checking it. A strap was cut on another piece, holding a suspended weight. On a third piece, the resistance bar gave way. The fourth piece seemed fine. Shey stopped and scanned the room. When her gaze met his, she pointed at him.

"You! Come with me. The rest of you are dismissed for today." She headed to Howell's office, with him beside her.

"I don't know what you thought you'd gain from this stunt but someone could have been hurt in there," she said as Howell's door opened.

"I put together the equipment the way it was supposed to be. I used it myself to make sure everything worked, following the holo-vid that came with it. I had nothing to do with what happened in there."

"Was anyone hurt?" Howell stood as they entered.

"Almost." Shey glanced at him.

"Can the problem be fixed?" Howell asked, looking at both of them.

"The equipment can be fixed," Berto began. "The problem is you have someone here that deliberately tried to harm someone else." He crossed his arms over his chest.

"What are you implying?" Shey shoved her hands on her hips, her brows furrowed.

"Did you lock the room when you finished, Berto?" Howell asked.

"Yes sir, I did."

"It wasn't locked when I checked on it last night or just now," Shey said.

"Then someone either broke in or let themselves in."

"That should be traceable." Howell opened his desk and retrieved a yav.

The three of them headed for the fitness room. Howell punched in the codes outside the door, but the door didn't lock.

Howell stepped inside and he followed, with Shey behind him. Howell felt along the inside of the doorframe and pulled something out.

"What's this?"

A small piece of metal, the size of a quarter-credit was wedged between Howell's fingers.

"You were right, Berto. Someone did this intentionally."

Howell applied the codes from the inside and this time, it locked.

"Can you get on the repairs today, Berto?"

"Yes sir, after my last class."

"How do we know Berto didn't tamper with the equipment?"

He glared at Shey. "I may have been a thief in my past, Shey, but I'm no liar. I didn't tamper with the equipment."

"Shey, if you have a problem trusting Berto, I suggest you supervise his repair work." Howell looked at him, then Shey.

"Let's keep this information between the three of us for now, until I can figure out who is behind it." Howell patted his back.

"Yes sir."

"You have time before the noon meal to start on the repairs," Shey said.

He glanced at his chrono, then at her before heading out the door. Without a word, he headed down through the eating hall. She kept up behind him.

When he stepped through the hissing door to go outside, CO Derek handed her the frequency code she needed to contact her father on Chroma.

"Thanks, sir."

By the time she got out the door, Berto had already stepped into the storage building out back. She raced to the entrance and stepped inside. Berto swung around so fast he bumped into her, knocking her to the ground. Except she didn't hit the ground. She felt his arms around her, cradling her protectively, yet one of his hands held a bag of tools, the other grabbed a shelf to keep himself from falling. She hovered a few inches off the floor. When he regained his footing, he dropped the bag and helped her up.

"I am so sorry, Shey. I didn't see you there."

"What just happened?"

"What do you mean?" He picked up the bag of tools.

"How did you keep me from falling? I felt your arms around me, but you didn't touch me."

"Believe me, if I had my arms around you, you'd know it." He held her gaze.

Yes, she wanted to feel those arms around her, but what other way could she explain it?

"What are you doing here, anyway?"

"I'm supervising your repair efforts, remember?"

"Ah, yes. Try to keep up." He hurried out the door and didn't look back once.

He had long strides and it took all she had to keep up without trotting behind him.

Once inside the fitness room, she watched him re-attach the malloid objects that held the weights. He replaced the straps with newer pieces on one machine and then repaired the damage to the third piece of equipment. When he finished, he checked his chrono.

"We have time if you want to try out the equipment."

"I think I will, thank you." She went to the piece with the weights first and adjusted it to her strength. After completing ten repetitions, she went to the next piece and did the same, until all three pieces checked out.

He stood back, watching her, but close enough to spot for her. At least he learned something in today's class.

"The fitness equipment seems to be functioning properly."

"Of course it does. It functioned properly the first time, too." He crossed his arms over his chest. His muscles strained the fabric of his shirt.

"Was that before or after you and Tam spent some time together?" She stepped a little closer.

"What?"

"You heard me. Someone could have been hurt today."

"Yes. The question is, who was the intended target?"

She narrowed her eyes at him. She didn't like what he implied.

"I had nothing to gain by hurting anyone, Shey. However, maybe someone in the class does."

She ignored his comment. "How can we prevent this from happening again?" Her arms felt awkward at her side.

"You'll have to keep the door locked at all times, making sure it's locked properly. You, the Commander and I are the only people who know the codes for that door. Go to Howell and have him set up a new code that only you two know."

"Then you wouldn't have access to the room."

"Right. And I would be blameless if anything else happens."

She glanced at her chrono. "It's time for the noon meal."

"I'll leave first so you can check the lock." He stepped in front of the hissing door.

"Berto?" Her heart hammered at what she needed to say.

He paused, his back to her. "Yes?"

"I..I owe you an apology."

He turned to face her, his arms crossed.

"I fully intended to come back and help you with the equipment last night but I let the time get away from me. That was the first party I had been to in several anos."

"It would have been a first for me too."

"I'm sorry for that. You shouldn't have had to do all that work yourself. And..I'm sorry I let anger cloud my thinking."

Berto stepped closer. "I forgive you."

"Why did you spare my life on Chroma?" She bit her lip and held her breath, afraid of what he might say.

"Because...you intrigued me." He turned and walked out the door without looking back.

6

When Berto entered the eating hall, the small talk stopped and people stared. His body hungered for food but his brain craved sleep. He slipped into the food prep room and grabbed a plate from Tabon.

"Hey! Where are you going with that?" Tabon asked, stunned.

"Outside. I'll bring the plate back, I promise." He exited the back door of the food prep room, which led to the garden area. He climbed upon the boulder near the pond and ate his meal. He didn't think he could make it through the next two classes. He wanted to be alone. He was used to that, after all. Alone with his thoughts was better than being with the others right now.

When he finished eating, he glanced at his chrono. A short nap would help. He took his plate back to the food prep room and washed it, along with his eating implements, and set them in the sanitizer.

He walked through the eating hall, his head down. He

wouldn't look at anyone. After today, maybe the class would forget his outburst.

In the hall, Tibu stood with a few others, talking about the incident in class.

"There he is," Tibu said, turning toward him. "How do you sleep at night?" he taunted.

He stepped aside to avoid the man, but Tibu grabbed his arm.

"I'm talking to you, Tarsian. How do you sleep at night?"

Tibu stood several millikiks taller than himself. He looked at Tibu's hand on his arm and clenched his teeth. He tightened his gut and radiated heat in his arms, burning Tibu's palm and Tibu withdrew his hand quickly.

"One of those Chromian girls you abducted recently was my sister. How do you live with yourself?"

He glared at the man, but didn't answer. What could he say? He knew the taste of revenge. There was nothing he could do or say to appease the man.

"You are yuka dung," Tibu said, taking a swing at his face.

He ducked Tibu's fist. A surge of power flowed through him as he straightened to his full height. Tibu's eyes widened. He shoved Tibu's chest and Tibu flew across the room. Tibu stared up at him in shock.

He walked passed past the others, heading to his quarters, but froze at the sound of Howell's voice.

"Berto, a word with you, please."

He turned back and realized the entire class had witnessed the encounter with Tibu, including Shey. Howell stepped over Tibu and went to his office. He followed in silence.

He rubbed his forehead. If only he could rub out the exhaustion, and all the events that led up to this moment.

"Have a seat," Howell said.

He sank into the soft chair. "If you want, sir, I'll go willingly to Plumaris to finish my punishment. You don't need me here anymore."

"Nonsense. Semm told me what you said in class today."

"I'm tired, sir, it slipped out."

"Look, Berto, only a few of us know about your past. We had planned to keep that secret. If you wish to divulge that information, that's your call. I'm afraid these are the consequences of others knowing about your relationship with Dram."

"Yes, sir." He clenched his teeth. Now, even more people will come forward for revenge against him. First Shey, now Tibu. He couldn't hide, not from everyone.

"Do you want me to talk to the class about your situation?" Howell asked.

"I don't think it will help, sir," he said, his head down.

Howell leaned back in his seat and crossed his arms over his chest. "When were you going to tell me about that gift of yours?"

Shey reached out and helped Tibu off the floor. "Your sister was not harmed during her captivity," she said to him.

"How do you know that?" He asked.

"Because I was there. I was abducted along with your sister."

"You were the instructor who allowed him to take all of you against your will?" Tibu's face grew in anger.

"I didn't allow him anything. I had no choice. They had weapons. If I fought against our captors, someone would have been hurt," she explained. Her mind went back to that day, seeing the events clearer than before. Four men aimed laser rifles at her and her students. Sure, she could have fought Berto for her safety, but what of the others? If she had been killed, there would have been no one to look after the girls, to keep them calm, and to help organize their escape when Genesis had been captured with them.

"Part of your fitness training will be learning how to escape when someone holds you against your will," she said.

"And part of the class training will be learning when that is not an option," Danner added, patting her shoulder.

"Escaping your enemies has more to do with opportunities than physical strength," Danner said, looking at the crowd that had gathered. "We will begin our lesson in five minutes," he said, guiding Shey away from the crowd. "You are welcomed to join in the class, Shey."

"I just might do that," she said, excusing herself.

Danner was right. The opportunity to escape was not present at the time of her capture. What she didn't tell Tibu was that Berto confided in her that everything would be all right if she kept the girls calm. There had been something in his eyes that told her to trust him. But what made her argue with the man every time they were together? At her rescue from Vestra Minor, she had wasted valuable time arguing with him. Then this morning, she had let her jealous anger control her in punishing him and his quarters-mates. For what? If she was to become an officer, she had to act like one.

The door hissed open to her quarters. She retrieved her comm-pad.

Berto was a complex man. And what he did to Tibu puzzled her. She had heard the other Tarsians talking about some legend. Was it true? Did he have powers of some sort?

Her door opened and she stepped into the hall, running

into...Berto. Without thinking, she grabbed him and brought him into her room, locking the door.

Berto rubbed his forehead. "Now what? I'm tired Shey. I have no energy left to argue with you."

She tossed her comm-pad on the bed and grabbed Berto around the neck and kissed him on the lips. She felt an odd shape in the back of his neck.

Instantly, he wrapped his arms around her, crushing her to him and deepening the kiss. She moaned and Berto kissed her passionately. His arms moved up and down her back, sending fire to every nerve ending. With one hand, she explored his thick, brown hair, the other, his back. She wanted this man more than she realized. She had fantasized about him since her rescue. When he pressed his hips against her, she realized he wanted her as well. She pulled away, slightly breathless.

"Ummm...I wanted to thank you for putting together all that equipment for me." She drew her hands to the front of his shoulders.

"I told you, I'm willing to do anything for you," he said, his arms still around her. "I meant it."

"And I'm sorry for being so...inconsiderate concerning your...welfare this morning."

Berto pulled her tighter against his body and kissed her neck. An explosion of sensations hit her hard and she gasped in pleasure.

"Apology accepted," he whispered, kissing behind her ear and moving his way down her neck.

Breathing became difficult. She should stop him. On second thought, hell no.

Berto's kisses trailed down her neck to her throat, blasting her with sensations that hit her core. She clung to him.

"We...ummm...have a class," she whispered, breathless and dizzy from his touch.

He leaned his head against her forehead. "I know," he groaned hoarsely.

"We'll continue this discussion later this evening," she spoke softly in his ear.

"I can't wait."

7

Berto slipped into the classroom and sat in the back, a renewed energy built up inside. If he could concentrate long enough on what was being said, he might learn something. All he could think about, though, was Shey.

Danner talked about opportunities and how some situations could become deadly without a plan. He was right. There had been too many incidents where someone tried to be brave and had been shot. Luckily, he hadn't been the shooter.

Shey slipped into the seat next to him. She was more composed now than she was a few moments ago. He glanced her way. He couldn't wait to finish their discussion tonight, if he could stay awake until then. Sitting next to her and not being able to touch her was too much to bear. Whatever had possessed her to come on to him like she did was fine with him. He would take all he could get. He didn't know what it felt like to be wanted, but this afternoon came pretty close. He would savor those feelings and emotions.

Danner continued his instructions on opportunities to

escape from captors. When he finished, Shey slipped out of the room before the others saw her leave. The class took a break before FI Bover came in to give his instructions on navigation.

"Berto, your eyes are red," FI Bover said, coming toward him. "Are you all right?"

"No, sir. It's sleep deprivation, that's all. Are you covering anything I don't already know?"

"That depends. Have you ever flown before?"

"Yes, sir. I piloted class A wing ships and wedges, along with class C cargo ships and transporters."

"Catch up on your sleep. But I expect you to be here tomorrow so I can test you on the simulators."

"Yes sir. Thank you, sir." He scooped up his comm-pad and headed to his quarters.

Thankful for the chance to get some sleep, he kicked off his boots and fell into bed. Thoughts of holding Shey helped him drift off to sleep.

Tibu complained of his treatment by Berto to two other recruits as Tam walked by. She stopped and approached the three men.

"Instead of complaining about it, do something."

"Like what?" Tibu asked.

"Make him pay for what he did to your sister...and to you."

"How?"

Tibu's lack of imagination angered her but she could use him easily. "Are you forgetting what LEO Danner taught us about opportunities?"

"What has that got to do with anything?" one of the recruits asked.

She glanced around then moved closer to the group. "You hurt him the same way he hurt you. But you must wait until the timing is right."

Tibu half smiled and nodded. She doubted he really understood her point but at least she planted a seed. She would have to do a lot of watering to get anything growing but it was worth it. She headed for her quarters to change before the evening meal. All this thinking made her hungry.

Once inside her quarters, she plugged her frequency module into the comm-pad and called her father, Che.

"He's here," she said, when his face came into view.

"Are you sure?" He looked doubtful.

"He's from the Denoy sector. I think he's the one the legend speaks of."

"The Incanta legend?" His eyes widened.

"Yes. I saw him use his power twice."

"Be careful. You know what he did to Mendo." Che rubbed his chin.

"How could I forget?" She glanced at her chrono. "I must go. Ask Jara if he's located the sister. I will call you later." Che's image vanished as she pulled the module from the comm-pad. Hurriedly, she changed for the evening meal.

Shey looked for Berto at the evening meal, but didn't see him. Her excitement at what would become of their relationship soon turned to disappointment.

"Have you seen Berto?" she asked his quarters-mates.

"No, not since before the last class," Telik said.

"Is anything wrong?" Coz asked, suspicious.

"No, I had a question to ask him, but it'll wait," she said. She sat with Danner, Bover, Semm, Howell and Lander.

"How did the first day go?" Commander Howell asked everyone.

"I've got a lot of work cut out for me if I want them in shape," she said.

"They ask good questions," Bover added.

"You know, I was thinking of combining your teachings on opportunities, LEO Danner, with some real-life practice on escaping captors in my second class tomorrow."

"Great idea!" LEO Danner said. "When they try to rescue the captives, they just might have to remember this training."

"We could do this a few times to refresh their memories before training is over," she said.

"I'm pleased with the way you are all working together," Commander Howell said. "We've only got six weeks to turn these people into I.S.P. agents."

"They seem eager to learn, sir. I think we can do it," HCO Semm added.

"That might change when they get to actual flight training," FI Bover said. "In two weeks I should know who will become pilots and who will crew."

Shey's mind drifted back to when she and Berto sat together on the transporter after her rescue. He hadn't minded her falling asleep against his shoulder. He even put his arm around her to make her more comfortable.

His recent warm kiss was sweeter than she imagined. The strength of his embrace made her feel safe. But when he kissed her neck, she lost all control of her senses. And if she hadn't been so mean last night, she could have danced with him.

She glanced around the eating hall. Tibu talked to his quarters-mates. He had been mad at Berto earlier when he discovered Berto had been one of his sister's abductors. She couldn't blame him for his anger. Looking back, his sister had never been in real danger, but she didn't know that at the time.

She finished her meal and after excusing herself, she headed back to her room. Seeking Berto again would seem questionable to others. She had to keep her distance as an officer and an instructor. Besides, he was Tarsian and she was Chromian, two races that didn't mix. That alone would cause her problems.

She sat on her bed and worked on her homework for officer's training when the door buzzer sounded.

Tam spied Tibu walking alone down the hall and joined him.

"Hello," she began. "How about taking a walk with me?"

"Sure," he nodded.

Tam and Tibu slipped out the door at the end of the hall near the storage closet. Walking in the dark around the building gave them a little privacy.

"Have you thought about what I said earlier?" She gazed up at him. He was taller than most Chromians, forcing her to crane her neck.

"Yeah. I want to hurt him, but you saw what he did to me."

She nodded. Yes, the Tarsian legend was true. Hurting Berto would not be easy. "So what is your plan?"

"I don't have one."

"Can I make a suggestion, then?" She couldn't help smiling.

"Sure."

Shey's door hissed open and Berto stood in the doorframe. She pulled him into the room, locking the world outside.

Berto folded her into his arms and kissed her so tenderly, she melted against him. When she came up for air, he assaulted her neck with kisses, sending sensations down to her core. Her fantasies became possibilities as she kissed him back, stripping off his shirt for better access. Mmmm, he was built. His chest tasted salty with each kiss.

Without a word, Berto carried her to the bed. Shoving her comm-pad out of the way, he gently removed her clothes, stopping long enough to kiss each breast thoroughly before roaming down her belly. Her skin reacted to each touch in anticipation. Within minutes, her possibilities became reality as he had his way with her. First, with dexterous fingers, he had her panting and wanting more of him as his touch drove her insane with need. Then, a talented tongue drove her over the edge as her body shuddered in release. Finally, his swollen shaft entered her body and Berto's rhythm made her shudder again as they both came together in a final climactic release.

Berto lay sprawled across Shey's warm body. This is where he wanted to stay...where he finally belonged. Did he deserve her? No, but he wanted her just the same. He rolled onto his back, pulling Shey on top of him.

"I've wanted you since the day I met you," she said.

His heart still pounding, he couldn't believe her confession. "You mean, even more than your freedom?"

"If it meant staying with you, I could've given up my freedom."

"Why did you give me such a hard time, then?"

"I don't know. Something about you just makes me want to argue with you."

"I never thought I... I don't deserve you."

"No, you don't, but you're mine."

"What happens now that we're mated?"

"We can't say anything to anyone until after the first mission. It would jeopardize my career as an officer. I don't know how it will affect you, but I don't want to lose you. Not after we..."

He kissed her passionately, exploring her sweet mouth with his tongue. Shey returned the kiss, and his body responded immediately. Only this time, she assaulted him with kisses, moving slowly down his overheated body. He let all his energy flow through him, amplifying his need and their passionate climax.

"Wow!" He snuggled against her, totally satisfied.

"Berto?"

"Yes?"

"What is that in the back of your neck?"

He reached for the spot. "Just a souvenir from some pirates long ago. They paid me to steal a cargo ship, but Dram got on the ship while I was stealing it and black-mailed me into working for him."

"Does it hurt?"

"Only if I press against it."

"I have a confession to make."

He held his breath as he watched her face, propping up on an elbow.

"When I first realized you were here, I wanted revenge against you, but this is my revenge." She propped herself up and kissed him tenderly at first, then passionately.

He returned the kiss and squeezed her tight.

"I forgive you for abducting me." She kissed him again and he reciprocated.

He moved a strand of blonde hair from her face and tucked it behind her ear.

"What I'm really here for, besides starting a new career, is searching for my brother's killer."

"How did he die?"

"He was killed on Tarsius fourteen anos ago in Denoy."

8

Early the next morning, Berto awoke to a blaring sound. He sat up in total darkness, remembering the sobering revelation from the night before. He had been the one who killed Shey's brother. How could he tell her that truth when she just forgave him for abducting her and changing her life?

"You going to turn that off, Sags, or do I have to do it for you?" Telik growled.

Sags pounded the alarm into submission. An illuminator went on.

"When did you get back?" Sags asked.

"I don't remember." He hoped there wouldn't be any more questions.

"We missed you at the evening meal." Telik jumped from his bunk.

"Yeah," Coz replied. "Officer Shey asked about you."

"Did she?" He slid his legs over the side of the bed and noticed an unfamiliar soreness. A slight smile escaped his lips at the memory, but his heart filled with dread. How could Shey ever forgive him for killing her brother?

"Did you get enough sleep after the all-nighter you pulled?" Sags asked.

"Yes, thanks," he lied. "Uh, men, if I make you uncomfortable being your quarters-mate, I'll be glad to leave." He had to clear the air about his past. He didn't want to drag his quarters-mates into Tibu's revenge issue.

"What are you talking about?" Telik asked.

The other three exchanged glances while getting dressed.

"We all have a past, Berto," Coz said.

"Yeah, and you did what you had to do at the time," Telik said.

He glanced at Telik.

"Howell told us how you came to work for Dram," Telik added.

"He told everyone?"

"Just us," Sags said, "since we are quarters-mates. He offered to move anyone who didn't want to remain in here with you."

"And?"

"You're stuck with us, Berto," Coz said.

Relief washed over him and the feeling of finally being accepted. He stood, stretching. "I promise I won't let you down."

"Let's hope not. We know where you live," Telik said.

"Thanks." He hurried to the cleansing compartment to freshen up before the morning workout.

Shey appeared happier than he remembered and put the class through the warm-ups. She introduced an exercise to escape would-be attackers, using him to demonstrate the technique. When he ended up on his backside, he realized that if the slaves had used this one technique, they never would have been captured in the first place. They all tried it, using a partner as a victim then taking turns until everyone could do it.

He wanted to kiss her so badly it hurt. But what hurt more was the truth about her brother. Did she know what kind of person he really was?

Today, he managed to get a decent breakfast with the others. Tibu and his quarters-mates brushed past him on the way through the double doors, nearly knocking him over.

"That was no accident," Sags said.

"Yes, I know," he agreed, but he was in no mood to deal with the likes of Tibu and Tibu wouldn't rest until he got his revenge. He would have to avoid him as much as possible.

He got through the history and cultures class with no problem and looked forward to Shey's second class.

Later, inside the fitness room, everyone broke into smaller groups to use the equipment, and those who waited became spotters. Shey stood in the middle, watching that everyone used the equipment properly.

Tibu pulled back on a weight and something snapped, bringing another weight slamming down toward his neck. Berto reached out with his mind holding the weight above Tibu to keep his neck from being crushed. Tibu jerked up, then rolled out from underneath.

Tam screamed.

"You, son of a holeach!" Tibu took a swing at him, but he halted Tibu with his own hand, covering Tibu's fist, crushing it with his normal strength.

"How could you do that?" Shey demanded.

"Do what?" He released Tibu.

"You nearly killed him," she said.

"I did no such thing," he insisted. "You saw me put this equipment back together. You even tested it."

"It's funny how everything worked fine a few minutes ago," Tam said.

He glared at Tam. What was going on here? He glanced down at the equipment and noticed a loosened rod. He moved toward the equipment.

"I think you need to leave," Shey stepped in front of him.

"What? There's a loose rod," he gestured.

Shey pushed his chest. "Now."

Berto saw the hurt and anger in her eyes. "I didn't do it," he whispered, then left the room.

He couldn't believe what just happened. How could she think he would stoop that low after what they shared last night? He was stuck here, though, whether he liked it or not. He was so angry he could punch something, but he had a job to do. Unfortunately, he had to get through the training along with everyone else.

There was an hour left, so he went outside and ran another three miles. He wanted to run until he couldn't run anymore. Maybe he could run until he was too tired to think.

He slipped into Danner's class late and sat in the back unnoticed. He listened to the lecture and took notes on his comm-pad. As soon as Danner announced a break, he was out the door so no one would notice he had been there.

He slipped through the eating hall and grabbed a plate from Cower as he handed it to Tabon.

"Is this going to be a habit with you?" Tabon asked.

"Uh, yeah." He exited the door. He would rather eat alone than deal with the others. He sat on the boulder once more and enjoyed the solitude. This time, he would purposely be late for class to avoid any altercations. He stretched out, enjoying Vaedra's warming rays with his eyes closed until a shadow fell across his face.

He opened his eyes to see Shey standing in the path of Vaedra.

His heart thudded in his chest. If only things could be like they were last night.

"What did I do this time, Shey?" He sat up, expecting bad news.

"I find it hard to believe that after what transpired last night you would dare to endanger the lives of any of my students."

"I find it hard to believe that you would even think I would do that. I hadn't been in the fitness room until that incident. As far as Tibu goes, I can't help that he hates me for abducting his sister. That's something I can't undo. But I won't stand there and let him attack me."

"You didn't let me finish," she said. "I don't know who is doing this, but it appears that you are being set up."

Stunned, he stood facing her. "Have you told Commander Howell?"

"Yes. He's changed the codes on the door but it was unlocked when I got to class today. He suggested that perhaps you should do your workouts at a separate time than with the class."

Berto ran his hand through his hair. "Do you think the sabotage will stop?"

"Well, if it doesn't, no one will be able to blame you for it."

He looked at his chrono. Class began one minute before. "Well, it's been a pleasure, Shey, but I've got a class. I'll do my workouts in the evening, on my own. That way, I won't be a distraction to your class."

Shey touched his arm. "I over reacted earlier because I was upset. If you hadn't been there, Tibu would have been seriously hurt. Thank you."

He nodded and hurried off through the food prep room. Being isolated from the class was bad enough but seeing the hurt in Shey's eyes tore at his heart. He couldn't bear the thought of hurting her further by telling her the truth about her brother's death.

After the class ended, he managed to slip out once more before the group and grabbed another plate from Tabon. But where would he go? Shey already knew about the garden. He headed for the landing pad.

Pressing the panel near the hatch, he climbed into the Galatin and sat at a window on the far side of the ship and ate in peace.

He leaned back in the seat and waited until the food prep room and the eating hall were cleared out.

He closed up the ship and headed inside. He cleaned his plate and left it in the sanitizer, then headed for the fitness room.

The door hissed open at his approach. Hmmm. Someone left it this way to gain access, but who?

He worked out the routine Shey had showed them but memories of her soft skin and firm muscles took his concentration away from the exercise. Afterward, he headed to his quarters.

No one was inside. Most likely, they were in the lounge where there were gaming tables, entertainment vids and music. He lay down on his bed. Training was going to be long. He wanted to get it over with. Maybe doing hard time on Plumaris wouldn't be so bad. At least on Plumaris, he would know who his enemies were—Dram...and everyone else.

Shey headed for her quarters after the evening meal. She thought about who would be mad enough at Tibu to hurt him?

Once inside, she pulled up the database that LEO Danner had given them earlier in class. He had showed them how to look up a person's profile to see if they were on the Law Enforcement Watch List. The LEWL was the only way someone could be tracked for their crimes in the Vaedra System. If they had been judged, then it would show their punishment.

She tried another tactic, typing in planet Tarsius, then Unsolved Crimes in the search bar. When that came up, she added the date fourteen anos earlier, and her brother's name. In moments, two other names came up: Mendo de Che and Jara de Vito. The other two were from Eloy sector, Tarsius. Mendo died days later from head trauma. Jara was uninjured.

"Hmmm." She needed to talk to Jara. Maybe she could convince her father, Kaal, to speak to him. Then she noticed a flashing red light at the prompt. She clicked on the light and another screen popped up. A message appeared: Case recently closed. How can that be? Kaal should have been informed of this. Fourteen anos had gone by without a word. On a whim, she went back to the search bar and typed in Mendo de Che. Suddenly, files flashed on the screen of her comm-pad. A photo of Mendo, before his death, popped up. He looked familiar. His black hair, dark brown eyes and tanned skin reminded her of...Tam. She read the files on

Mendo. He had been caught for stealing when he was eight and again at ten anos and had to repay what he stole and do community service for an ano in both cases. When he was twelve, he assaulted a younger girl and tortured another one. He had to repay both families with supervised labor for an ano, along with community service. At fourteen, he assaulted a girl of seven. After that, the file was marked DECEASED.

The file on Jara showed that he was involved with the same crimes as Mendo when he was twelve and again when he was fourteen. He liked torturing younger girls as well. The fathers of the two boys were brothers.

She typed in the names of each father. Jara's father was serving a life sentence on Plumaris for murder. Mendo's father had assaulted women and spent a lot of time working community service for it. He currently ran a gambling estab-lishment in Eloy.

She typed Kalen ni Kaal in the search bar. Her breath caught when Kalen's picture came up. He wouldn't be on this list if he hadn't committed a crime. Kaal was right. She swallowed hard before reading his record.

Kalen ni Kaal had assaulted younger girls on Chroma when he was ten and again when he was twelve. At thirteen, he had stolen some property and assaulted another girl of thirteen. He repaid the first two families with supervised labor and community service. The third family he repaid with money and never served his community. At fourteen, he assaulted a girl of seven. His file was also marked DECEASED.

Her stomach churned at the thought of her brother assaulting girls. Kalen had always been good to her. She couldn't imagine him hurting anyone. Kaal had taken Kalen with him on long trips with his shipping business while she stayed behind with her aunt. After Kalen's death, her father taught her to fly cargo ships. Until her teaching assignment on Chroma, she had always thought she would go into the shipping business with her father. Kaal was the one who talked her into becoming a teacher, like her mother had been.

She set her comm-pad down and inserted the frequency module. Wiping her eyes, she called her father.

"I read Kalen's profile," she choked out the words.

"You should let it go, Shey. What's done is done." Kaal shook his head.

"You were right, Kaal. I didn't know Kalen at all."

"I gave him more chances than he deserved, Shey. Did the report show what he did before he died?" His face hardened.

"He assaulted a girl of seven. How could he do that?"

"He didn't just assault those girls, Shey. He raped them. They were going to send him to Plumaris when we got back, but he never made it." Kaal closed his eyes briefly.

"I didn't know he was such a monster. Why didn't you tell me?"

"You were only seven when he died, Shey. I didn't think you would understand what he was accused of at that age. You always looked up to him but I never left you alone with him because of that."

"It said the case was recently closed but it didn't say who killed him or the boy with him."

"There was another involved?"

"There were two others. One died from head trauma. The third boy survived."

"Shey, it was worse than I thought. Three boys and a girl of seven? Was the girl...did she...survive?"

"It didn't say, Kaal. If she survived, she could have been

traumatized. It sickens me to think about it. I had a student not much older than that at the Academy. She was such a sweet, trusting girl."

"After all these anos, Shey, I want to put his memory to rest. I don't want to talk about him again."

"I need closure, Kaal. I want to know who killed Kalen and hear his side of the story. I want to know what happened to the girl."

"Is that all, Shey? Or are you still seeking revenge?"

"I'm in shock, Kaal. I'm not sure what I want anymore." She clicked off and unplugged the module. Her heart hammered her chest. She had a lot to think about tonight.

The next morning, she showed the class another exercise to escape an attacker, then reviewed the previous day's training, before sending everyone out on a five-mile run.

Berto kept his distance. She hated that she could only see him in one class but she had to see if the sabotage would continue with his absence. Afterall, it was Howell's idea. She followed behind on her own run, making sure no one cheated.

Today Berto kept up with his quarters-mates. It was best she kept her distance, physically and emotionally. She couldn't jeopardize her job as an instructor and officer.

After his run, Berto ate his morning meal alone in the food prep room, where Cower set up a small table for him.

"Why are you doing this?" Tabon asked.

"I'm trying to stay out of everyone's way," he said.

Cower and Tabon shook their heads.

He couldn't figure out why the equipment in the fitness room was tampered with a second time. Who would do that, and why? Was he the target? Or did they want to blame him for it? If he hadn't been in there, Tibu would have been killed.

He checked his chrono. The group should be in the fitness room now. He headed for the simulators instead.

"Trying to get some extra time in, Berto?" FI Bover asked.

"Yes. I thought I would finish as much as possible before class."

"I hear you've been making yourself scarce."

"I'm getting my work done. I'm just trying to stay out of trouble," he said.

Bover leaned on the sim that he'd turned on. "Look, you have this stuff down. I'll sign off on your work and you can do whatever you want instead of sitting in on my classes."

"What do I do in the meantime, sir?"

"I'll check with HCO Semm and LEO Danner. Maybe there's something you can help them with."

"I doubt it. I actually learned something new in their classes."

"Honestly, I don't know why Commander Howell is putting you through these classes. But you have a point. They may cover some things about the I.S.P. that you don't know. Maybe Commander Howell will let you do the weapons training on your own."

"I'm familiar with the weapons the I.S.P. uses. Who teaches the weapons class?"

"Commander Howell."

"That figures."

He finished his simulation work and watched FI Bover sign the certification.

"Let me know when we do the actual flight testing, sir."

"Of course. You'll be the first to know."

He headed out of the class and into the lounge to wait out the class change. He would do the fitness class while the rest of them were in flight training. As long as he could avoid them, he would be fine.

Howell was speaking to Shey in the fitness room when he walked in.

"Uh, sorry." He turned and headed back out.

"A word with you, Berto," Howell said.

Great. "Yes, sir?" He spun around and walked toward the two of them.

"Do you have any suspicions about the second equipment failure?" Howell asked.

Shey looked down at the floor.

"No, sir, I don't."

"Come with me," Howell put his arm around him and turned him back toward the door. When they got outside in the hall, he led him to his office.

"Berto, I feel you've been through a lot of similar training when you worked for Dram."

"Yes, sir." Bover must have spoken to him.

"Your specialty was systems technology, wasn't it?"

"Yes, sir, I trained with Ignacio on Tarsius and on the job working for Dram. I've worked on a lot of different classes of ships."

"Well, I'd like you to get our ships ready for our first mission."

"Ships, sir?"

"Yes. We'll be getting four class-A wing ships in this week. All used, of course, but it's a start."

"Yes, sir."

"I'll have Danner and Semm set up your assignments so that you can do them on your own. Shey will check with you on your fitness levels by testing you periodically. Bover has already signed off on your sim work. He informed me that you could actually teach what he's doing."

"Yes, sir." Berto smiled. He owed Bover for that one.

"Sir?"

"Yes, Berto?"

"Thanks, sir."

"I know it's been awkward on you, Berto, but I can't afford to lose someone of your caliber. Good agents are hard to find."

"Thank you, sir." He hesitated. "There's one more thing, sir."

"What's that, Berto?"

"The last time I worked out in the fitness room, the door was unlocked. I thought you and Shey were the only ones with yavs to the room."

"We are."

9

Berto worked out a routine that week with Semm and Danner. After running with his quarters-mates, he grabbed his meal then headed out to the landing pad to work on the ships.

He had pulled out some wires from the Nav-u-com when he felt a presence. He glanced over his shoulder, but nothing was there. He sat up and visually searched the navigation room. When that turned up nothing, he went throughout the ship and found no one there.

He scratched his head. It was a definite presence of some sort, but he couldn't figure out what it was. He headed back to the navigation room and continued where he left off.

He took his breaks in the ship and went over the material he got from Danner and Semm. He got a yav from Commander Howell in the evening and worked out in the fitness room while the others hung out in the lounge or did laundry.

"I thought I'd find you in here eventually," Shey said, slipping inside the fitness room.

He continued pumping his weights, trying to ignore her.

"You know you have to report to me weekly," she said when he didn't respond.

"I report to you every morning when I run. If you have something to say to me, you can do it then. This is my own time." He set the weights down and moved to another piece of equipment. He lowered the bar over his shoulders and behind his back. Trying to focus on exercise, while Shey stood in front of him, was difficult.

"Turn your wrists like this," she said, touching his hands and angling his wrists slightly. "Doesn't that feel better?"

Just her touch affected him. How did she do that? "Are you finished?" he asked, clenching his teeth.

"Not quite," she said, crossing her arms and moving around him.

He raised a brow, hesitating with his weights. He wanted things the way they were the other night.

"I get the feeling that you are trying to ignore me."

He continued to work the back and shoulder muscles by pulling down on the weights. "Why would you think that?"

"Well, because you are making yourself scarce."

"I thought that was the point so that the equipment isn't tampered with."

Shey closed her eyes momentarily. "I miss you."

His throat went dry. He missed what they had but how could he continue this relationship, knowing what he did to her brother? "Have you and Howell changed the codes again on the fitness door?"

"Howell gave me new codes this morning."

"Well, the door was unlocked today. I even got a yav from Howell, but that was pointless."

Shey glared at him. "I lock it every time I leave this room."

"Well, someone has been coming in here and tampering with the equipment, but it hasn't been me."

She turned away and checked each piece of equipment for any signs of sabotage.

"Everything appears to be in order," she said, approaching him. "I take it that the weights you're using are working fine."

"What do you think?" He stood up. He had to get away from her. He wanted to stay mad. He was used to people being mad at him. He grabbed his towel and wiped his forehead as he approached the door. He felt along the side of the door panel, but there was nothing there.

"You better figure out how they're breaking in here, otherwise someone could get hurt."

"I came here to ask your help," she said.

"Oh?" He moved on to another piece of equipment that worked the thigh muscles.

"Since I've been here, I've been doing some research," she began.

"On how many ways you can get revenge on a slave trader?" He watched her reaction while pumping his legs against the weights.

"I admit the thought crossed my mind, but that was before I forgave you. I got my revenge, remember? I've been researching how my brother died fourteen anos ago."

His heart did a double flip before beating again. His mouth went dry and his throat parched as he swallowed hard, pumping his legs slower now.

"While my father waited for his shipment in Eloy, Kalen took leave. Hours later, he was found dead in a cave in Denoy."

He froze. His nightmare returned. The hatred he felt toward the boys who held down his sister, while Kalen forced himself on a frightened girl of seven overwhelmed him. He closed his eyes and tamped down the energy that flowed through him. He had to control it before it controlled him. He clenched his fist and tightened his jaw, taking in a deep, calming breath. He slowly let it out before he could look Shey in the eyes.

"I thought, maybe you knew something about it, since you're from Denoy."

He slowly nodded. What would he say to her? He lowered his head. He couldn't look her in the eyes.

"Tell me what you know." She moved toward him, resting her hand on his thigh.

Her touch seared him like a brand, but he didn't move.

"Have you read the reports?"

"Yes, I have, but it didn't tell me who killed him or what happened to the victims."

"Victims?"

"There were...other incidents involving my brother. He made reparations for his crimes except for the last one. I want...closure. I need to know what happened to the little girl."

"The little girl went to a healer. Her physical wounds healed instantly, but it took many visits before her mind was healed." He stood.

Shey's mouth dropped open and her eyes widened, while his heart pounded in his chest. Shey reached for his arm. "Was she...your sister?"

He nodded then left the room as his heart broke in two.

. . .

Shock washed over her at the realization that it had been Berto's sister. She raced to her quarters and pulled up the LEWL on her comm-pad. This time, she searched for Berto's name. Her pulse hammered while she awaited the information. Images flashed on the screen, finally resting on Berto's face. She read his file.

Berto de Alberto, caught stealing food at age eight and again at ten. No parents, but supporting a young sibling, he offered labor as repayment and later was exonerated for the crimes.

Arrested for assisting in Slave Trading under Dram, and confessed to stealing two class A wing ships, a class C cargo ship, a class C transporter ship, and two class A wedge ships, which were returned to their owners. He confessed to the self-defense killing of Kalen ni Kaal for the rape of Mariposa de Alberto, age seven. Of the two accomplices, one, Mendo de Che, later died of head trauma. The other, Jara de Vito, is serving time in Eloy's detention facilities.

Berto was exonerated for the deaths in that both boys were minors and a healer testified to Mariposa's injuries.

Shey slumped over her comm-pad. Her brother was a monster.

And Berto, the man she fantasized about, and mated with, was her brother's killer. Her heart hammered in her chest while bile rose up in her throat. She remembered Berto's comments in Howell's office. He wanted to check on his sister to make sure she was all right. His concern for his sister touched her.

But how could she forgive the man who killed her brother?

· · ·

Berto lay on his bed, his arms clasped behind his head. The only woman he ever cared about could never care for someone who had killed her brother. The ache in his chest grew at the thought that after finding a mate, he would lose her forever.

He wouldn't hide from his attackers, and he wouldn't run. He could defend himself if he had to, but prevention was much easier on everyone.

He sat up in bed. He would confront Tibu about his revenge. The matter with Shey could wait. He headed for the lounge. He wanted to get this over with. It was better to know who your enemies are than to pretend they don't exist. At least that's what Dram had taught him.

"Tibu?" he called out across the gaming tables.

Tibu straightened to his full height and glared at him. "What is it you want?"

"I told you I worked for Dram for four anos against my will. It was his way or death. I chose to do things his way, until I escaped."

"Why are you telling me this?" Tibu asked.

The room was filled with recruits, along with some of the staff.

"I want to know what kind of revenge you seek against me," he said.

"Revenge?"

"Yes. You've tried to hit me on more than one occasion. Are you going for torture? Do you want to kill me? Or are you planning on annoying me for the rest of your life?"

Tibu's face grew angry as all eyes focused on him.

"I...I..."

"Think about it and let me know. Otherwise, leave me

alone." He turned and left the room. He headed for his quarters. Now that the threat was out in the open, maybe he would have peace. If Tibu decided he wanted revenge, everyone would know about it. He would no longer hide from the others to keep the peace. He was tired of hiding.

As he reached Shey's quarters, he hesitated. He pressed the buzzer on her door panel.

The door hissed open and Shey stood in the frame.

"What kind of revenge do you want, Shey?"

"What do you mean?"

"Would you feel better killing the man who killed your brother? Or do you prefer to torture me for the rest of your life?"

"I'm not sure what I want."

"Think about it, Shey. And think about what you would've done if you were in my place." He left Shey to her thoughts.

10

———

Berto, Coz, Sags, and Telik ran together the next day.

"Nothing was said after you left," Telik said.

"Any trouble from the instructors?" Coz asked.

"Bover signed off that I've completed his course, but I'm working individually with Semm and Danner. While you are all doing your second workout, I meet with them and get my new assignments."

"What about your second workout?" Sags asked.

"After the evening meal, I work out on my own," he said.

"Has Shey given you any more trouble?" Sags asked.

Shey and Tam ran together, not far ahead. He enjoyed watching Shey move down the makeshift track. She was graceful, athletic, and muscular. Thoughts of having those muscular legs wrapped around him sent a warm shiver through his body.

"I gave her the same challenge last night," he said.

He heard a low growl before the screech, then something jumped out at Shey and Tam from the daga weeds. He stopped the kabor with his thoughts and forced the large animal backward, flipping it over. The kabor ran off.

He ran ahead to see if the women were all right. Shey and Tam had fallen over trying to get out of the path of the kabor.

"What was that?" Shey looked up at him. He reached a hand out to pull her up. Coz helped Tam to her feet.

"That was a kabor." He glanced over his shoulder to make sure they were safe. "They usually stay in the Nica valley."

"Why would it come here?" Shey asked, brushing the dirt off her clothes.

"Because you two looked like easy, tasty targets," he said.

"I can't blame them a bit," Coz added.

He shook his head and hid his smile. But the thought had occurred to him as well.

"Maybe we could run in larger groups," Shey suggested.

"Or we could start carrying weapons," Telik added.

The men exchanged glances. He didn't need a weapon, but if everyone was spread out, he wouldn't be able to protect them all.

"Let's finish together," Shey suggested.

There were at least three smaller groupings of four each spread out across the track. The students had picked up running together in quarters groups. After today's excitement, that could change.

The track was one mile in circumference, so it was easy to keep up the distance, but some people ran faster than others. There was no way around that.

Shey had brushed up against him while they ran. Coz and Sags struggled to get on her other side, but Coz won. Telik and Sags kept up a conversation with Tam.

"I want a word with you after the run," Shey said to him.

His heart skipped a beat. He couldn't tell by the request if she was mad or relieved. Hopefully, she'd thought over his proposition from last night. He didn't know if she would remain civil toward him. He couldn't take another heart-ripping.

After the run, the small group broke up and headed for the eating hall. He remained behind.

"You wanted to see me?" he asked.

"Yes. I thought about what you said last night, and I want justice for Kalen's death."

"Fair enough, but the I.S.P. felt I was justified in what I did and exonerated me after their findings on Kalen's records."

"That won't bring Kalen back." Shey clenched her teeth and put her fisted hands on her hips.

"No, but it will save other girls from the same fate as Mari."

Shey lowered her head. "I'm sorry your sister had to go through that."

He reached out and gently squeezed her arm. Her sincere apology touched his heart. Moments later, he heard the familiar growl and screech.

He turned in time to see the kabor leap at his face. He swirled around, shoving Shey out of harm's way, his back toward the kabor, and forced the animal to the ground where he choked him to death with his mind. He must be more careful in the future. Shey's sadness had distracted him.

He had been caught off guard, just like the time Ramen shot him, and it almost cost him his life.

"Oh, Berto, you're hurt," Shey said, turning him around to check his back.

Within minutes, most of the recruits were outside.

"Are you all right?" Telik asked.

"Yeah, I'll be fine," he lied. The burning pain was intense now.

"Take your shirt off," Shey ordered.

He pulled the fabric over his head, and felt the cool air sting his back. He hissed.

Shey splayed her warm hands across his back. "I need to get you cleaned up. Come with me."

"Hey, is this thing edible?" Cower asked.

He shrugged. "That's the first one killed around here."

"Come on, men, help me get this to the building. Tabon will have to help me skin this creature," Cower said.

Once inside, several recruits followed Shey and him back to the eating hall.

Tam and Tibu were inside, along with Tibu's quarters-mates. No one spoke but they all watched them walk through the eating hall and through the double doors.

Shey led him to the fitness room, where she retrieved her healing kit.

"Sit."

He sat on a bench while she applied anti-germ wraps to his skin. He hissed at the coolness. Why did she even bother if she wanted him dead?

Shey knelt down behind him and lightly patted the wraps against his back. "I'm sorry you got injured," Shey said.

"I was distracted. It won't happen again."

"How can you be so sure?"

"I can sense when there's danger."

"Really? How about when something is good?"

"What do you mean?"

"I think the two of us would be good together," she said.

"Us?" His heart skipped a beat. "I thought you wanted justice for your brother. If you seek justice, there is no 'us'."

Shey gently applied more wraps. "There could be 'us'."

"Not unless you can forgive me, Shey."

He felt her hand stiffen against his back.

Tam, Tibu, Telik and Coz entered the fitness room as Shey finished applying the second set of wraps.

Sags entered with the rest of the class, while Shey put her healing kit back together.

"You need to let the wraps absorb the germs before doing any hard labor, Berto. Those were nasty wounds. I'll check on you later." Shey dismissed him and began assigning people to the equipment.

He headed out the door. Telik nodded at him, "Later."

He went to see Danner about his assignments, carrying his shirt in his hand. The cool air on his back, along with the medicinal wraps still stung, while chilling his body.

"Sure, Berto, turn in your assignment later today. I'll let Semm know your situation," Danner said, then reached out and grabbed his arm before he could leave. "When were you going to tell me about that power you have?"

He studied Danner. How could he explain the power he had inherited from his mother? "I think I was born with it. I'm still learning how to use it."

"What else can you do with it?"

"I can move things and...I can control the elements."

"What do you mean?"

He glanced around to make sure they were alone. "I can call on the wind and rain to cause a storm, or move the storm away. I can create dust storms or storms of fire."

"You're the one the Junali legend speaks of, aren't you? The son of Incanta?"

He nodded. "I prefer not to reveal that secret just yet. You and Howell are the only ones who know of it."

"The others saw you stop Tibu from punching you, twice."

"Yeah, but they don't know about the elements. I wasn't going to stand there and let him hit me. I know he's angry at what happened to his sister, but I'm not the only one who was there when she was abducted."

"Couldn't you sense that the kabor was about to attack?" Danner asked.

"I was...distracted."

"Shey?"

He nodded. "If he hadn't growled and screeched just before hitting me, I wouldn't have had time to stop him."

He headed back to his quarters. His assignments were on his comm-pad. He could work on them now and then get started on wiring the new ships.

Bover came around the corner. "I saw what happened this morning. Are you all right?" he asked.

"Yes, sir. I'm getting a little stiff. I could use a healer's touch right now," he said.

"Those healing wraps should do the trick. Hopefully, when Counselor Contor arrives, he will bring a healer with him. Commander Howell requested one for the compound."

He continued on to his quarters.

Once inside, he headed for the cleansing room. He gently pulled one of the wraps away from his skin to check the damage. A deep laceration caused from the kabor's claw oozed blood. He patted the wrap in place then concentrated on his energy. He drew all of it up to his center and focused it onto his back. He felt a warming sensation travel up and down his muscles.

Healing was something he had never tried with his powers.

After a few minutes, he pulled the wrap away from his skin. The lacerations were still there but appeared to be scabbing over. At least the burning stopped. He slipped a clean shirt over his head and went to work on his assignments.

Shey couldn't wait to get the class over with. All she could think about was the warm, firm muscles she had touched earlier. She chewed her bottom lip at the thought.

There was something about Berto that made her emotions flipflop. She had to get a handle on them. She needed to work on...discernment.

She'd told Berto she wanted justice for her brother's death. But could she forgive him? Tonight, she would contact her father. Later, she would check on Berto's back.

Commander Howell came down the hall behind her.

"A word with you Officer Shey."

"Yes, sir." She followed him to the office.

"I heard about the events this morning. Are you having problems with Berto?"

"Well, sir, I just discovered he's the man who killed my brother fourteen anos ago." Her pulse raced at the thought.

"Hmmm. That is a problem. How do you feel knowing this?"

"I had every intention of avenging my brother's death, sir, until I discovered some things about the case."

"Anything you care to share with me?"

Her heart rate kicked up a notch, so she sat down to calm herself. "My brother was not the boy I thought I knew, sir. He had some...aggressive tendencies toward women that I was unaware of. Along with two other boys he met while on leave, he attacked a child...Berto's sister." She lowered her head, the words caught in her throat. "I think it would be best if Berto continued to work out on his own."

"Agreed. And will you explain what went on between you and Berto this morning?"

"What do you mean, sir?" Now her heart pounded remembering the events.

"A lot of people saw your interaction with him. It looked like it was getting personal before the kabor attack."

"He gave me an ultimatum last night about my revenge issue. He asked me to think about what I wanted, whether I wanted him dead or just tortured."

"And?"

"I'm not sure, sir. I'm still trying to understand why my brother was...the way he was."

"It appeared there was something else going on."

"I apologized for what Mari, Berto's sister, had gone through. I think he appreciated the gesture, that's all."

"You do remember that officers are not to fraternize with the students?"

"Yes, sir." Thank God he couldn't read her thoughts.

"In light of the situation, and for your own safety, Shey, I feel it would be better to have another team member with you if you need to speak to a student apart from class."

"I...understand, sir." She stood to leave, then hesitated.

"I think we need some new yav codes for the fitness room, sir. If Berto no longer has a yav, someone else is breaking into the room."

"I'll correct that situation immediately," he said, calling PO Lander on the communicator.

·   ·   ·

When she left Commander Howell's office, her confusion about the man she had fantasized over intensified. She should hate him, but she didn't. The knowledge that he killed her brother numbed her feelings toward him. She'd wanted justice for Kalen, secretly wanting her brother's killer dead. She wanted him to suffer the way Kalen suffered. But what about the girls Kalen tortured? Learning how he operated apart from his family stunned her. How could she have lived with him and not seen the monster hiding behind those eyes?

Kaal had known. He had seen the way Kalen behaved. He had to face the accusers with Kalen since he was a minor. He kept that information from her because he knew how much she loved Kalen and she wouldn't understand at seven anos. That's why he took Kalen with him on so many trips, to keep him away from society. Kaal had said Kalen was a bad seed, like his brother. And her uncle Teldon served a life sentence on Plumaris. Kalen had been sentenced to Plumaris to serve time there when he returned home on Chroma. Only he never returned to Chroma. Maybe his death was a good thing.

Now that Commander Howell knew about her revenge issue, she couldn't carry it through. But how could she even think of revenge when Berto's sister lost even more that day? Her eyes watered at the thought that Mari lost her innocence and had to live with those horrid memories.

Shey wiped a stray tear from her eyes, not for her brother's death, but for Mari.

She stood in the hallway and checked her chrono. Soon it would be noon meal. Perhaps one of the instructors would go with her to check Berto's wounds?

The students were in class with Danner now, maybe...

Bover or Semm would be available. She headed for the instructors' quarters.

Knocking on Bover's door, she stood outside and waited, when Berto came around the corner with his comm-pad.

"Uh…how is your back?" she asked.

Berto half smiled. "Great."

"I was—"

Bover opened the door. He looked at her then Berto. "What's going on?" Bover asked.

"You go," she gestured, looking at Berto.

"Uh, I'm turning in my assignment, sir," Berto said, shoving the comm-pad toward Bover.

"Your turn," Bover said to her.

She felt her pulse kick up. "I need to check on Berto's injuries, but I was instructed to have a team member with me to do that."

"What?" Bover and Berto said in unison.

"There is talk among the recruits about…us." She gestured between her and Berto, while looking at Bover.

Bover crossed his arms and looked at both of them. "Well, is it true?"

"No!" she and Berto said in unison, almost too quickly. She swallowed hard, forcing herself to look noncommittal, while her heart said otherwise.

Bover continued to glance between the two of them. "Come in."

She and Berto stepped inside the room. Bover took Berto's comm-pad and connected it to his larger pad, downloading Berto's assignment. He went to his cleansing compartment and got his healing kit.

"Okay, you can check his injuries while this downloads."

Berto put his hands up in surrender.

"Sit," she ordered.

Berto grabbed the chair from the desk and turned it around, sitting on it backward. He pulled the clean shirt over his head and waited.

She took out the healing wraps from the kit and handed them to Berto. "Hold these, please?"

Carefully, she peeled each layer off Berto's strong, muscular back. The back she had kissed and touched not long ago. The back she wanted to caress and kiss again.

"Good God! Is that from the kabor?" Bover asked.

Berto nodded.

"If it hadn't been for Berto, I could have been killed," she said. "He stopped an attack earlier that would have killed Tam. We both owe him our lives."

Berto flexed his back muscles as she put the cool healing pads on his warm skin. She patted them on carefully.

"It looks like it's healing nicely," she said.

"How did you stop the attack?" Bover asked.

"I...um...used telekinesis."

Shey held her palm against his back momentarily. The warmth penetrated his flesh.

"How long have you had this...gift?"

"Since I was born, I think."

"There is a legend in Junali history that speaks of a 'hua-can', a person within whom dwells the forces of nature," Bover said.

"I am aware of that legend," Berto said.

11

───────

"The forces of nature?" Shey asked. Her hand rested against his shoulder.

"Yes, like a powerful storm, or quakes, or the oceans rising up, or the eruption of mountains," Bover explained.

"Legends are just stories," Berto said.

"From my experience, legends are born of truth that was elaborated upon," Bover said, while disconnecting Berto's comm-pad from his own.

Berto slipped his shirt on, while Shey packed up Bover's healing kit.

"Thanks, Officer Bover," she said, handing him the kit. "I think it would be best if I left first."

Bover nodded as she exited the room.

Why did this have to happen? One indiscretion and everything changed. At least she got to touch that strong, firm back of his. She remembered what it was like to feel his skin next to hers in a warm embrace, or to kiss his chest, his face.

She missed him.

The fact that he had power to move things was an interesting bonus. He saved her life, and that of Tam. That was a plus in his favor. She still had to decide whether or not she could forgive him. Her feelings toward him were still mixed. Finding a mate, as old as she was, was unheard of. If she chose not to forgive Berto, she would live a life of loneliness. Once mated, no one else would have her or Berto either. They would each endure the same fate.

Finding Berto here had given her fantasies a new hope until she discovered he was Kalen's murderer. And should she even have feelings for Berto after what he'd done? She had resented Kalen's killer for fourteen anos. Turning off that feeling would be hard, even if Kalen deserved it.

Her feelings for Berto started almost when she met him. Now that she thought about it, he intrigued her as well. The next few weeks would drag by if she couldn't see him without another instructor present.

She stopped at the fitness room and used the new codes and yav that Howell and PO Lander came up with and checked her own healing bag for supplies. Then she sat on a bench and planned her next workout session.

Berto headed for the ships and noticed the dark clouds in the distance. It didn't rain much on Meta, except over the valley area and in the mountains. He had three more ships to finish before the end of their training. The first ship would be ready within days. Most of the work he needed to do was minor upgrades to the system. But there had been a few wiring problems he wanted to attend to that just didn't seem right. He'd missed them the first day, but he was usually pretty thorough when he went through something.

He enabled the ship and did a systems check. That was odd. He looked at the red flashing light. Where was that malfunction coming from?

He retested all his systems and finally located a problem with the air support. He tracked the wiring back to its source and discovered the wires had been cut. He checked these the other day and they were fine.

"Hmmm."

He spliced the wires together and put everything back through the tests once more. This time, everything checked out. He finished up with the systems screenings then decided it was ready for a test flight.

He headed for Howell's office.

"The first ship is ready for a test flight, sir," he said.

"Good. I'll go with you, Berto," Howell said, rising.

Berto sat beside Commander Howell in the class A wing ship and watched Howell put her through pre-flight.

"Everything seems fine, Berto. Buckle up."

Within minutes, they were up and running.

"We'll take a short cruise around Meta," Howell said, as he pushed the throttle forward. The ship rose and headed into the rain.

While the craft hovered over the Nica valley, the power grid on the Nav-u-com flashed then went black. The wing ship dropped hard. Berto's gut rushed to his throat as the ship hit the ground, crashing near Anya pond. The rain poured from the sky. The force of the fall threw him and Howell against the Nav-u-com. His head throbbed instantly and something warm dripped in his eye. He wiped at it with his hand.

"What the Vaedran hell!" Everything checked out before the flight. He unbuckled his safety harness. "You okay, sir?" he said to Howell.

"Yeah. What happened?" Howell looked dazed.

"We lost power, sir. I checked everything before we left. This shouldn't have happened." He helped Howell out of his seat.

"Can you fix the ship?"

"I think so, sir." He headed out the nav-room door to the engine room to retrieve his tools. When he returned, Howell was sitting in his seat, leaning against the Nav-u-com.

"Are you sure you're feeling all right, sir?"

Howell glanced at him. "Head pains. I think I'll be fine once we get back." Howell studied him. "Your head is bleed-ing, Berto!"

He wiped at the throbbing and saw blood on his fingers. "I'll be fine, sir." He had been through worse pain than that.

"Help me with this panel, sir."

Howell helped him pull the faceplate off the Nav-u-com. He checked all the wiring. "Everything is fine here, sir. I'll go to the belly and check the engine systems."

He climbed down the steps to the engine room and pulled the panel covering the wires in the ceiling. They were all in good shape. When he traced the connections to the engines, there was a piece of adhesive sticking out.

"What's this?" He peeled it back and found a clump of wires had been severed and covered over with adhesive. He missed it before...or did he? He had gone over every connec-tion before he went to Howell.

He climbed up the steps. "Sir, you need to see this." He

motioned for Howell to follow, but didn't wait to see if he would.

Down the steps and to the connector, he pulled a light stick out to show Howell his discovery.

"You checked this before our flight, I take it," Howell said.

"Absolutely, sir. My life would be at stake, too, if I let something get past me. This was done when I went to get you for the test." He scratched his head and remembered what he'd found before.

"Something strange occurred earlier, sir. I found some wires cut after I had checked them the day before."

"They were cut? Why would someone do that?"

"It was to the air supply, sir. If I hadn't re-checked everything, we would discover it when we were in space and we'd be dead before we could get to safety."

"Let's see if we can get this back to the base," Howell said.

"I'll splice the wires for now, sir, but I suggest you let me re-wire the whole thing. You don't want something to go wrong once we are space-borne."

"I'll have to place some guards on this project," Howell said. "I'm not sure who I can spare...or trust anymore."

"Sir, I'll be glad to pull guard duty."

"Yes, but you've got to sleep sometime. I'll figure something out today. I'll see if I can communicate back to the base."

He hurriedly spliced the wires together, using the adhesive left behind to keep from sparking the wires. There was no reason for this to happen, unless...someone still wanted revenge.

There were only two people who came to mind, Tibu and Shey. But Shey said she wanted justice. Tibu didn't seem as if he knew enough about ships to pull this off, but Shey? Well, she did have a background in shipping. She had flown transporters with her father and brother when she was younger.

Why would she do this? Everything seemed fine a while ago in Bover's quarters.

Berto and Howell got the engines engaged and flew the ship back to the landing pad on low power.

"I'll have Jans, from communications, take first watch then Davmic can pick up the second. I'll find someone else to pick up third."

"What about me, sir?"

"I need you to work on the ships. We've got a few weeks left on training, then we head out on our missions."

"Yes sir."

"Wait here for Jans. When he shows up, take your evening meal and then work on this ship to get it ready for testing tomorrow. There should be some new wire in the storage unit."

"Yes sir." A few minutes later, Jans showed up.

He collected the wire and brought it back to the ship, along with more tools he would need. Then he headed to the eating hall.

He found a seat with his quarters-mates and sat down, noticing Shey was absent.

"We heard about the crash," Sags said. "What happened?"

"We were testing the ship for readiness." He didn't know how much Howell wanted the others to know.

"So, it's not ready, then," Coz said.

"You could say that."

"It looks like you got a nice cut to your forehead to show for it. How's your back?" Telik asked.

He touched his still-throbbing brow but the pain had gradually subsided. The gash was long and a scab had formed over it. "Much better. The healing wraps are beginning to work."

He remembered the tender way Shey had applied the wraps and wished Bover hadn't been there. But now, he wasn't sure he could trust her. What if it was Shey who severed the wires?

"I wish that had been me the kabor scratched," Sags said.

"Why?" Berto asked. Why would anyone want to be attacked by a wild, dangerous animal?

"Then I could get the extra attention from...Shey," he whispered.

He narrowed his brows at the man. "What are people saying?" Not that he cared, but he did want to make sure no one jumped to conclusions.

"Well, after you touched her arm, everyone started talking," Sags said.

"And?"

"They think something is going on—between the two of you," Coz added.

"Well it's not." he lied. "Three of Dram's men and I had abducted Shey and her class on Chroma. That's how I know her. She wanted to know who killed her brother. I gave her the information she needed. Her brother raped a small child and she...apologized for it. I thanked her for her concern, that's all. There is nothing going on between us." He stood, wishing it were otherwise.

"Maybe not physically," Telik said under his breath.

He ignored the comment and left the eating hall, clenching his teeth. Telik was right. It was an emotional thing. Now that she knew he killed her brother, there never could be anything more between them. That's what hurt the most. Could someone like him ever expect to be happy?

His quarters-mates hadn't done anything wrong, but he was so mad, he wanted to hit something. He tamped down his feelings to avoid his power from surging. At least he knew his anger caused the force of energy to flow. If he only knew how to control it, then maybe he could use it for good.

How could he stop the feelings that caused so much pain? The kiss he longed for and finally got would have to sustain him. For one brief moment, he knew what it felt like to be wanted, even if the woman did overreact. She couldn't deny the other night ever took place, and the way she felt in his arms promised more. Their future depended on Shey. Now they couldn't be together without a 'supervisor'.

Frustrated, he headed back to the landing pad. He had to get Shey off his mind. Jans stood guard outside the ship.

He started at the Nav-u-com and worked his way back to the connector in the engine room. He fed a few strands of wires at a time. It would have been easier and faster if he had some help with the wires, but if Jans helped, it would take him away from guarding the ship.

"Berto?" a soft, feminine voice called out.

He jerked up, hitting his head. Had he imagined Shey's voice? Rubbing the pain away, he re-opened the cut on his forehead.

"Berto?"

"Shey?"

"I'm outside."

He moved through the ship quickly to find her standing at the ramp. She held her healing bag and a stool in one hand, and a plate of food in the other.

"I brought you some food and came to change your healing wraps. Come outside and I'll be finished in no time," she said.

He complied, looking forward to her touch. "I've already eaten, Shey."

Jans stood nearby, his arms crossed. "I haven't."

"Here you go, then." She handed Jans the plate of food then placed the stool on the ground. "Sit here."

He obeyed, pulling off his shirt. He wanted to pull her into his arms and hold her against him instead. At her nearness, he smelled the sweet kiskis scent on her skin.

"Oh, goodness! You're bleeding," Shey said. She angled his jaw to see better, but held his face gently in her one hand while cleaning away the blood with a cleansing wipe.

Berto clenched his teeth with her nearness. Her soft breath blew against his face as she placed a small healing wrap onto his forehead.

"How did you get this new cut?" Shey asked.

"Didn't you hear about the crash?" Berto asked.

"What crash?"

"Howell and I crashed in this wing ship on a test flight today."

"Are you all right? How is Howell? Is he hurt?"

Shey sounded like she genuinely cared. Maybe she didn't know about it.

"Howell may need some attention. He seemed dazed after the incident."

Shey held his face with both hands now and stared into

his eyes. "And what about you? Are you experiencing any dizziness? Pain?"

He swallowed hard. His heart ached, but that didn't count, did it? "My head has been throbbing for a while but it's not as bad now."

"I have something for head pains." She let go of his face and the warmth dissipated. Shey searched through her bag and pulled out a small wand-type container. She applied the ointment around the wound, since it was now wrapped. "This should help with the throbbing. Let me know if you need more."

Shey moved to his back. She carefully peeled off each of the old layers, setting them on the ground.

"You are healing nicely," she said.

Jans glanced at his back.

"Ouch! That's got to hurt."

"You should have seen it when it happened," Shey said.

"Jans, how about helping me with some wiring when Shey is finished?" Berto asked.

"No. My instructions are to let no one aboard any of these ships except you."

"Why is that?" Shey asked.

"Those are my instructions from Commander Howell."

"Has something happened?" she asked, finishing up with his back.

"Let's just say we are preventing anything else from happening," Berto jumped in. "But helping me with the wiring will take only a few minutes. Otherwise, I'll be here all night."

"Sorry, Berto, those are my orders."

"I know something about wiring," Shey said. "My father taught me some things while I worked for him in his shipping business."

His heart thudded in his chest. Yeah, he wanted her in the ship...alone. Shey, knowing something about wiring, was a nice bonus, but could he trust her? Could he trust himself alone with her? And why would she even offer to help when she knew he killed her brother?

12

"Call Howell and ask him if I can have some help on this project," Berto said.

Jans tapped his communicator on his jacket. "Jans to Commander Howell."

"Howell here."

"Sir, Berto requests help with his project."

"Anything he wants Jans, I trust him. Just stay at your post. Howell out."

"You heard him," Berto said, pointing at Jans.

He strode up the ramp, pulling his shirt down over his back. Shey followed.

"Let me show you what I'm doing," he said, leading the way to the fusion engines. "I've got the wire started here." He pointed. "I need you to feed this through the opening. I'll catch it above and then feed it through the floor."

"Umm, Berto?" She picked up the end of the wire.

"Yes?"

"Thank you...for saving my life the other day." Shey licked her lips.

"No problem." He turned and climbed up the steps before it was too late. His heart pounded in his chest.

Topside, he rubbed his forehead. That was close. He wanted to pull her into his arms and smother her with kisses. But that couldn't happen. She wouldn't let it. Control, Berto, control!

"Now, Shey," he called out. Shey fed the wire through the opening. He found the end and pulled it out, then wove the loose end through the pipe under the floor, which was a straight shot to the Nav-u-com.

"That's the end," Shey called out.

He headed down the steps once more to connect the wires while Shey watched.

"Why did you volunteer to help me?"

"I don't really know, except I'm caught up on my work. Besides," she shrugged, "I had nothing else to do."

"What about your...supervised encounters with me?"

"Jans is outside. Doesn't that count?"

"He can't hear what we're saying, and he can't see what we're doing, so I don't think so." He glanced around for a tool that was on the far side of the engine room. He called it to him with his mind, reaching for it with his hand.

"I bet that comes in handy at times," Shey said.

"Uh, yeah. Tell me, Shey, am I the only one privileged to be supervised?"

"No. I'm supposed to have another team member with me whenever I need to speak to any student."

He glanced at her. "I get it. You're the one who is being supervised."

She glared at him as he stepped closer to her.

"I am not!"

"Should I be afraid of you?" He moved closer.

"Maybe you should." She scowled at him before moving around him. She climbed up the steps to mid-ship.

"If that's all you need Berto, I'll be on my way," she called out.

He moved up the steps and caught up with her. "Thanks for your help, Shey."

She turned and glared at him before moving down the ramp in silence. She grabbed Jans' empty plate and headed for the building.

He watched her walk back to the Comm room entrance and noticed Jans watched her as well.

"Women!"

"Yeah," Jans replied.

Jans glanced at his chrono. "I need to make my rounds. I'll be back in a few."

He watched Jans leave then headed back inside to finish the wiring.

He pulled the faceplate off the console, then peeled back the mastic and connected the first wire. He needed another tool and called out to it with his mind. He raised his arm and wrapped his fingers around the object when it touched his hand.

The memories of rigging Dram's ships for speed came back to him. Dram had avoided the I.S.P. for many years because Timna had installed power converters on all Dram's ships. Then, when he came along, Timna taught him how to do that.

While all the ships he had stolen had been returned to their owners, none of them had those power converters anymore. He had discreetly removed them before the I.S.P. could return the ships. But the power converters were still here on Meta.

He got up and headed for the storage building to search

for them. He didn't see why the I.S.P. couldn't be faster than the criminals anymore.

He searched through boxes of parts before finding what he needed. Emptying another box, he put the four converters and some extra parts inside and headed back to the ship.

When he approached the ramp, he realized Jans hadn't returned. He had been gone awhile now.

"Jans?" he called out as he climbed up the ramp. No answer.

He finished connecting the wires with the power converter attached. He ran some tests, clicking on the power switches and checking the readings. Green lights on all. Good.

He grabbed the scanner and went below to do a systems check.

Moving through the crawl space that went aft, he checked all connections using the scanner's checklist. Everything functioned properly. He missed nothing this time. Reversing directions, he backed out of the crawl space. No little feat with his large frame.

When he passed by the ramp again, he noticed that Jans was still missing. A bad feeling washed over him.

When he got to the Nav-room, he powered down and locked up the ship using the remote. He searched the pond area with no luck then headed to the other landing pad. The three ships sat waiting, eerily quiet in the dark.

He tried the remote on the first two ships, after searching around the exterior of all three. The remote wouldn't open the two hatches. Finally, the third one opened on the first try.

He climbed up the ramp and felt along the inside door panel for a light stick.

"Hmmm." A dark object on the floor of the ship caught his attention. He bent to pick it up. It was Jans' communicator. He tapped it on. "Berto to Commander Howell."

"Howell here."

"Sir, have you seen Jans?"

"Isn't he at his post?"

"No sir. He went to make some rounds almost an hour ago and hasn't returned."

"Where are you?" Howell asked.

"On the landing pad with the three ships."

"I'll be right there. Howell out."

While he waited, he checked inside the Nav-room. No one there. He checked the first sleeping compartment. Nothing. He went to the second compartment. Still nothing.

"Did you find him?" Howell was breathless coming up the ramp.

"Not yet, sir. I was about to check the cleansing compartment."

At his approach, the door hissed open.

13

———

I nside the cleansing compartment, Jans was face down on the floor.

"He doesn't have a pulse," Berto said.

"What?" Howell bent beside him and carefully rolled Jans over. "No apparent wounds." Howell tapped his communicator.

"Davmic, get central command. Tell them we have a K-14 and need assistance."

"Yes, sir."

"Davmic, after you contact central, get Lander, Bover, Danner, and Semm up here right away," Howell added.

"Why Lander, sir?" he asked.

Howell stood. "He's been through this type of investigation before."

Howell looked at him. "Tell me what you know."

"I worked on the wiring until Shey came to change the healing wraps on my back. She brought me some food, but I had already eaten, so she gave it to Jans. Afterward, she pulled some wire for me then left."

Howell raised an eyebrow.

"I needed help and she knows a little something about systems. After she left, Jans said he had to make his rounds. I never saw him again after that."

Four men came running toward them. Two carried a large case and set it down beside Jans.

"Not Jans," Lander said, kneeling beside the body.

"I'm afraid so," Howell said. "Tonight, everything goes on lockdown. Berto, you and CO Derek get on top of that. Curfew starts in ten minutes. When we get finished here, we'll meet in my office."

Berto left and headed inside through the communications room. Davmic was on the vid comm with central.

"Who was it?" Davmic asked.

He lowered his head. "Jans."

"No! I was supposed to relieve him in twenty minutes," Davmic said.

Berto glanced at his chrono. "We go to lockdown in eight minutes. Sound the alarm and use the intercom." He reached into the weapons cache and pulled out a couple of stun weapons and several locks. He strapped on a holster and shoved one laser inside, then headed to CO Derek's quarters.

He pressed the buzzer on his room. The door hissed open.

"This better be good," Derek said, holding a shirt in front of an otherwise naked body.

"Uh, CO Derek, Jans is dead and we're on lockdown. Orders from Commander Howell. He wants us to handle the lockdown, sir."

"What other officers are in the building?"

"Officially? Only you, sir. We'll be meeting in Commander Howell's office as soon as they finish outside."

"I'll be right out." His door hissed closed. Moments later, Derek emerged in his unicrin.

Berto handed Derek the second laser and some locks.

"Let's check the food prep room first," Derek said.

Inside, the room was neat and clean but empty of people as it should be. Berto went out the back entrance and set the lock then re-entered through the communications room. Derek bolted the door to the food prep from the eating hall. They continued out into the hallway, where the alarm still sounded and Davmic made his announcement.

Derek walked toward the lounge, but the door opened and several men poured out into the hallway.

"Hey, what's going on?" Coz asked.

"Lockdown," Berto said.

"What's that?" Tam asked, coming up from behind them.

"Everyone is to return to their quarters for the night."

Tam looked at her chrono. "It's still early," she said.

"Orders from Commander Howell," CO Derek said. He looked into the lounge and motioned for them to leave. When the last man was out, Derek set the lock.

They checked the office, classroom, and fitness room, which were empty. Then the two headed to the officers' quarters. "We'll save these for last," Derek said.

Tam's room was at the end of the hallway. He pressed the door buzzer.

"Yes?" Tam stood in the doorway.

"Anyone in here with you?" he asked.

"No, but you can join me if you like," she offered, leaning against the doorframe in a provocative pose.

Derek shook his head then punched Tam's outer door panel, clamping a lock on it.

Berto raised his hands in surrender when Derek glanced at him. Then they headed for the men's quarters. Berto waited outside the room while Derek went inside checking to make sure everyone was there.

"What's this all about?" Tibu demanded.

"You'll know in the morning," Derek answered.

"Why isn't Berto locked in his room?"

"He will be, eventually." Derek stepped out of the room and then locked the door panel from the hall entrance. They did the same routine for the next room before moving on to his room.

"I can't lock you in with them, since Commander Howell gave both of us the orders to do this."

"Well, we'll lock them in until we know what Howell wants to do with me. Let me check on them first." He went inside.

"What's happening?" Telik asked.

"I can't say much right now because of the investigation, but someone was killed tonight."

"Killed? Who was it?" Sags asked.

"One of the staff. That's all I can say right now. You'll know more when Commander Howell wants to tell you." He left. Derek locked the door and the two of them moved on to the last of the quarters.

The last room was used for the food prep people, Lander, Davmic and Jans. Cower and Tabon were the only ones inside, so they locked it, along with the laundry facilities, storage room, and outside entrance before heading back to the officers' quarters.

"That's everything but the officers," Derek said.

"And everyone, except Davmic and PTO Shey, is with Commander Howell," Berto added. "Should we lock the officers' quarters?"

"Yes. We can always unlock them later." Derek started with the first room and made sure it was empty before locking it and moving to the next. When they finished, he and Derek headed to Shey's quarters.

He buzzed her room and the door hissed open.

"Excuse us, PT Officer Shey, but we're on orders from Commander Howell to lock down Meta Station."

"What's going on?"

Derek glanced at him and he answered.

"Jans is dead, Shey."

"What?"

"Everyone here is a suspect, PTO Shey."

She glanced at both of them. "Is there anything I can help you with?"

"We'll let you know when Commander Howell gets back." Derek pressed the door panel to close it before locking her inside.

Berto swallowed hard at the thought that he and Shey were the last two people to see Jans alive.

"We need to get back into food prep," Commander Howell said, approaching him and CO Derek.

He unlocked the door and stood aside while Danner and Lander carried Jans' body to cold storage.

"This will have to do until the investigation is over," Commander Howell said. "Everyone to the office."

Within minutes, he and all the officers, except Shey, stood in Howell's tiny office.

"Berto, I know you aren't staff, but you've been here the longest. You know this place and some of the equipment we use. I want you to take turns with Davmic in communications for now."

"Yes, sir."

"Bover and Semm will take statements from everyone in here tonight. We can use the classroom and the office. I'll need this for the investigation."

"Yes, sir," Bover replied.

"We've locked PT Officer Shey in her quarters, sir, if you need her assistance," Derek said.

"I may need her later to take a watch. Danner and I will take the first watch. All watches will be in four hour shifts. Lander and Shey will take the second, Bover and Semm the third shift. Derek, I'll need you at communications in the morning."

Berto sat with Semm and gave his statement, then headed to communications.

"Davmic, I'm your relief tonight," he said. "Fill me in on what's going on."

"The investigations unit from Central I.S.P. will arrive around 1800 hours tomorrow. Counselors Thebes from Vestra Major and Contor from Tarsius will arrive with them."

"How many people are coming?"

"Oh, I figure at least ten," Davmic said. "They're coming on a military, class B Escort ship." Davmic handed the headset to him. This night was going to be long.

Shey paced inside her quarters. She couldn't believe the news about Jans. How could this happen? First, the fitness equipment had been sabotaged not once but twice. Then someone tampered with the ship Berto had worked on, and now this. In all three cases, Berto was involved. He said he had nothing to do with the equipment problem, but what if he did? What if he was a good liar? He had Howell fooled. He was the one who wired the ship that crashed. Who else knew he was working on it besides Howell? But why would he kill Jans? What did he have to gain from all this?

Maybe he was getting his revenge for being captured by the I.S.P.? Or maybe he was trying to set someone else up and got sloppy.

Her thoughts drifted back to the night of passion that they shared. Everything about him seemed sincere, yet she still had doubts. He said he would do anything to make it up to her. He took her punishment the night of the party and put up the equipment all by himself. He took the punishment she dished out when he was exhausted and didn't complain. And he genuinely cared for his sister.

But how could she forgive him for killing her brother?

Her buzzer sounded, bringing her out of her thoughts. When she approached the door, Bover stood on the other side.

"I need to ask you a few questions. Come with me." He headed toward the classroom and she followed. She sat down with Bover while he made some notes on his comm-pad.

"Where were you tonight after the evening meal?" he asked.

"I was late to evening meal. Everyone was gone so I went back to my quarters and ate some fruit that I had saved from morning meal."

"Why were you late?"

"I had been working on my lessons for tomorrow and finishing my officer training work that I lost track of time."

"So what did you do after that?"

"I remembered Berto's healing wraps needed to be changed so I went to the fitness room to retrieve my healing kit and some fresh wraps. Then I checked the locks that Commander Howell and PO Lander installed on the door panel."

"After that?"

"I passed Davmic in the hallway and he said he was relieving CO Derek for a few hours because Jans was called to special duty outside with Berto. So I walked with Davmic to the Comm room where I ran into Tam. She carried a plate of food. I asked her where she was going with the food and she said she was taking it to Berto."

"Then what happened?"

"Well, Davmic took over for CO Derek and I offered to take the food to Berto because I needed to change his healing wraps."

"So you brought the food to Berto?"

"Yes, and I grabbed a stool from the Comm room. But when I offered the food to Berto, he said he had eaten and since Jans was hungry, I gave him the meal."

"Was Tam with you?"

"No. While Jans ate the meal, I changed Berto's wraps outside the ship, in front of Jans."

"And did you leave immediately after you treated him?"

"No." Her pulse quickened at the question.

"Why not?"

"Berto requested help with the project he worked on. Jans said he couldn't leave his post, so I volunteered."

"Why?"

Now her heart pounded. She didn't want to lose her job over her indiscretion with Berto. She really had wanted to see him but she couldn't lie, either. She swallowed hard before answering. "I helped my father wire his ships one summer to save kashis. I thought I could help, so I volunteered."

"Didn't you realize you were breaking Commander Howell's orders?"

"Jans was just a few feet away while I pulled wires for Berto."

"And did you continue to help Berto after Jans left his post?"

"No! Jans was still there when I left. I was there just a few minutes."

"That's all for now, Shey," FI Bover said, making notes on his comm-pad.

Her heart hammered so loudly she swore FI Bover heard it too.

Tam read in her room when she heard the door buzzer. A few clicks later, the door hissed open. Officer Bover stood in the doorway.

"Well, isn't this a little late for class?" she asked.

"I'm here to get your statement. Come with me."

She followed Bover out the door and down the hall.

"And what statement is that?" She followed him into the classroom where they sat at one of the tables.

Bover tapped his comm-pad on.

"Well, come in. Have a seat while you're at it," Tam said sarcastically, gesturing with her hands. She crossed her arms over her chest.

"Where were you tonight after evening meal?" Bover asked.

"Gee, I think I went straight to the lounge," she said, tapping her chin with her fingers.

"How long were you there?"

"Until the lockdown, I was there all night." She uncrossed her arms. "What's this about?"

"Is there anyone else who can corroborate your story?"

"Everyone who was in the lounge."

"And who was in the lounge with you?"

"Let's see." She tapped her chin once more. "There was Tibu, Zed, Crocker, Coz, Telik, and a few others. I can't remember everyone. Some came and went. Most of us played stickit. When someone lost, they usually left."

"And you didn't leave the lounge until lockdown, is that it?"

"Pretty much. Oh, I did have to relieve myself once, and then I came back."

"Did anyone go with you?"

"No. I can relieve myself all by myself, thank you."

Bover clicked off the comm-pad. "That will be all for tonight."

"What about tomorrow? Will classes be at the regular time?"

"We'll let you know tomorrow." Bover stood in the doorway. "Let's go."

"Wait! You didn't tell me what this is about."

"It's an investigation. Tomorrow you will know what it's about, now, back to your room. Let's go."

Tam got up and followed Bover back to her quarters, where he locked her inside.

"Tozat-brained wombit!" Did he think that lock could keep her in her room? She leaned against the wall beside the door panel. With an investigation and the place on lockdown, she couldn't be caught outside her room. She would wait it out, like everyone else.

Four hours later, Shey heard her door buzzer. Howell stood at the entrance.

"It's your watch, Shey."

"Four hours isn't enough time to sleep."

"No, it isn't, but we don't have much choice now. You'll be working with Lander, patrolling the halls and periodically checking the grounds. Here's your laser weapon. You'll need it outside. Kabors, remember?"

"How can I forget?"

Lander came around the corner as Howell left. "I just checked all the locks."

"Now what do we do for the next three hours and fifty-nine minutes?"

"We could make our rounds outside. Together."

"Together is good. After what happened to Berto yesterday, I wouldn't go out there alone in the dark."

She and Lander headed outside with their laser weapons drawn and ready. Berto had the watch in the Comm room.

Being outside in the middle of the night was eerie enough, but the noises she heard were frightening. It smelled wet, like a recent rain. She shined the light stick on the ground. The gray dirt was spotted like drops of rain marked where they fell.

"That's the first rain we've had since we've been here, isn't it?" she asked.

"I think so. This is a desert area. Most of the rainfall goes into the mountains or the valleys where the ponds are located," Lander said.

They checked the ships to make sure they remained locked, then patrolled outside the building.

"I never realized there were only three windows on the whole building. I wonder why."

"Maybe Dram didn't like windows," Lander said.

"Maybe. But someone could walk around the entire building without being seen. I would expect Dram to be more vigilant when he knew he was a wanted man."

Lander stopped in his tracks and stared at her.

"What?"

"Why would you say something like that?" Lander asked.

"Look around you. It's true. Maybe someone slipped out of the building and killed Jans then slipped back inside without being seen."

"That sounds more like what happened when the ship was sabotaged." Lander said.

"Yes. The question is, who is doing all this and why?

14

———

Tam sat with her legs crossed on the bed, her hands resting on her knees. She inhaled deeply, humming an ancient chant.

Calm, deliberate planning. Until the training is over and the assignments are made, there's no need to rush things. She would wait. She had waited fourteen anos, what were a few more weeks? One little surprise turned up, though. Distraction dulled the senses. She would use that, taking advantage of his weakness.

On the other hand, Shey would be much easier to work with. Jealousy spurred her to action. That was her weakness.

Berto scanned the vid-screen, checked the monitors, and listened for incoming messages. He had three more hours to remain awake. He'd much rather be with Shey, finishing what they started.

Her watch coincided with his, making it harder to

concentrate, but then, there wasn't much going on at this hour.

He concentrated on sending large waves of energy to caress her then sent smaller waves aimed at her core.

A loud buzzing pulled him from his thoughts, as Shey and Lander came through the outer door.

"See anything on the vid-screen?" Lander asked.

"Nothing but darkness."

"Berto, are there any security cameras in place around this building?" Shey asked.

"There were when Dram was...when this was his base. I'm not sure about now."

Lander glanced at Shey. "That's a good idea, Shey." He turned to him. "Berto, turn on the cameras."

Did he miss something? He didn't know what idea they talked about, but he glanced over the controls near the vid-screen. The cameras showed they were on, but there was no vid-feed on the monitors.

"They're already on. Let me check something." Berto flipped some buttons and the two monitors on either side of the vid-screen flickered to life. Each screen showed two different scenes.

Lander and Shey moved close behind him, studying the screens.

"Can you tell if the cameras recorded anything?" Shey asked.

He glanced at her and realized what her idea was. He searched the panel of buttons and located the switches that controlled the camera facing the ship he had worked on. He figured out which one he needed to return to earlier in the evening and flipped it on.

Images appeared on the screen. Jans stood outside the

ship near the ramp. His arms crossed, he visually scanned the area.

Moments later, Shey walked toward him. She had a plate of food in one hand and her healing bag and stool in the other. He saw himself walk down the ramp. You could see the conversation taking place, but there was no audio. Shey handed Jans the plate and Jans began eating, while he watched himself take off his shirt.

He remembered the feel of Shey's hands on his flesh while he watched her remove the healing wraps and replace them with new wraps.

While they watch the vid-feed, he noticed the time stamp on the bottom of the screen. "Look." He pointed when the screen showed Shey walking up the ramp with him. Jans set his empty plate on the stool and moved closer to the entrance, looking inside. About fifteen minutes later, Shey emerged, angry, and left. The feed showed him and Jans watching Shey walk away. Shortly afterward, Jans left to make his rounds. Nothing unusual happened.

He flipped more switches and pulled up the vid-feed from another camera angled at the second landing pad. It showed Jans going up the ramp of the first two ships and coming down moments later, holding his light stick then closing up each ship. When he went up the ramp of the third ship, a dark figure appeared and entered the ship. Moments later, the figure jumped down from the ramp and the ramp closed. Jans never came out.

He sped up the vid-feed, but nothing else happened until he watched himself try to open each ship with his remote and not succeed until the third ramp opened. The rest of it played out with Howell and then the others.

"Can you go back to the feed that shows the figure going into the third ship?" Lander asked.

He pushed more switches to get the vid-feed back to the frame that showed the figure. Then, searching the panel, he found the one button that paused the frame, and a knob that enlarged it. Because of the distance of the camera to the ship, the image was not clear, but the figure was dressed in dark clothing from head to toe.

"He's taller than we are," Shey said.

He glanced up at her. He knew Shey was six centikiks because they were the same height. Lander was taller than all the recruits, but this figure had to duck to get inside the ship. All ship entrances were 6.5 centikiks.

"If it's a recruit, he won't be hard to find," Lander said.

"I have a record of everyone's height and weight for measuring their success rate in my class," Shey said.

"Can you get that information now?" Lander asked.

"Yes." Shey left the Comm room.

"How did Shey come up with this idea of checking cameras?"

"She noticed the lack of windows and suggested how easy it would be to slip around without being seen," Lander said.

"Maybe I can find out who sabotaged the first ship."

"Go for it."

Berto searched the vid-feeds of the cameras on the right side of the building and realized they recorded only twenty-four hours at a time. "I wonder if these feeds are saved anywhere."

"If not, then we need to figure out how to save that one before it's too late."

He typed in 'files' on the processor and pulled up a vast amount of information. "It'll take me awhile to sift through all this."

"Maybe I can get you some help." Lander dashed out of the room.

Within seconds, Shey walked in. "Where was PO Lander going in such a hurry?"

"He went to get me some help. I have too many files to sift through to see where these vid-feeds are saved. We aren't sure they're saved at all and we don't want to lose the feed we just saw."

She set her comm-pad down on the desk and leaned toward him. "Shortly before PO Lander and I entered this room, I felt the strangest sensations in my body—"

"Let's see what you've got, Berto," CO Derek said, coming into the room.

That was close. He now knew how he could affect Shey, whether she liked it or not.

Berto got up from his seat and pointed to the files. He filled Derek in on what they found with the vid-feeds and cameras.

"Dram was more high tech than I thought," Derek said.

"Yes, that's what impressed me the most when I started working for him. He had to be one step ahead of the I.S.P."

Shey shook her head. "What he did was wrong. How can you two talk about him like that?"

"Well, Shey, if it wasn't for Dram, I never would have met you and none of us would be working here, now would we?"

Her mouth dropped open as Derek chuckled.

"He's got a point, there," Lander said.

Shey exhaled heavily through her clenched teeth. It was all he could do to keep from laughing, too.

"I don't suppose any of you are interested in seeing who our suspects are?" She powered on her comm-pad then scrolled down a list. She pointed to a couple names. Berto glanced at her list: Tibu and Kar. Of course.

"Tibu's at the top of my 'People to Avoid' list," he said.

"Howell will need that information for his investigation," Lander added. He glanced at his chrono. "I guess we need to make our rounds of the halls."

Lander and Shey left the Comm room.

He moved behind CO Derek and watched him work with the files.

"I should have checked all the equipment out when I got here. I didn't realize there were actual cameras in place around the compound."

"Dram didn't want to be caught off guard. He always had a backup plan. Unfortunately for him, his son convinced me we were better off without Dram. That's when I learned what teamwork was all about." And he gained a friend in the process, something he never had before.

"I think I found the files," Derek said, "inconspicuously labeled by the dates."

"Well, that makes it easy. Let's take a look at the other day." He waited as Derek brought up the files. Each date had eight sub files, one for each camera. Once Derek figured out the numbering system, he brought up the vid-feed they needed.

They watched as he walked up the ramp of the ship. It was some time before he came back down the ramp and headed for the building. Another dark figure came from behind the ship and moved quickly up the ramp and went inside. The figure came back out shortly afterward and disappeared behind the ship. It was a minute or so before he watched himself and Howell come out of the building and go up the ramp.

"It's not the same person. This one is much shorter."

"Who's much shorter?" Shey asked, coming in with Lander.

"The person who sabotaged the ship," Derek answered.

"The person who cut the wires knew where to go and what to cut to disable the ship," he said.

"Did you get a look at the face?" she asked.

"Too dark and too far away. All we could tell was this person was much shorter than the other."

Before long, Semm and Bover came in and replaced Shey and Lander.

"Why don't you get some sleep, Berto. I've got it for now," Derek said.

"Sure."

"And thanks."

He glanced at Derek, puzzled.

"It wouldn't look good on my part if the investigators came in asking for this information and I didn't know we had it."

He pointed a finger at Derek. "You owe me, then." He headed for his quarters. "FI Bover, I'll need you to lock me in, sir."

Bover followed him to the room and unlocked the door.

"If you need me, you know where I am."

"Remember to keep quiet about what you discovered tonight."

His quarters-mates were asleep, so he quietly crawled into bed. Since Shey had recently gone to bed, he thought he'd have a little fun with her before drifting off to sleep. He concentrated on sending waves of caresses over her body, while he pictured himself caressing her in person. Then he sent smaller waves aimed at her core, gently moving his fingers in the air. He smiled as he drifted off to sleep.

.   .   .

Shey had just gotten to bed when that strange sensation overtook her again. It started at her neck and moved down her body, over and over again. The feeling was pleasant and relaxing while faintly stirring up passions inside her.

Was Berto doing this? It felt so much like the way he touched her the other night. She gave in to the feelings, letting the soft caresses float over her. When they stopped, another caress took her by surprise. It was stronger and deeper than the one she experienced earlier. This one had her writhing in her bed from the pleasure. She bit her hand to keep from screaming, but soon she panted from the intensity, until it suddenly stopped. She let out a breath, exhausted.

Berto was one talented man, she had to admit. That's another point in his favor.

A couple of shifts later, the I.S.P. contingency arrived, along with Counselors Thebes and Contor. The investigation began that evening. Recruits were singled out and interviewed extensively in Howell's office.

Jans' body was removed from cold storage and taken on board the Escort ship where he was put through a full body scan to determine cause of death. Fluid samples were taken as well. The lab on the ship was large. The medtechs went through everything carefully, studying all the samples that Howell and the others retrieved the first night.

The next morning, classes resumed as usual, except for Berto, who continued to help CO Derek and Davmic with their eight-hour shifts. Other than classes and meals, everyone was still on lockdown. The extra staff from the Escort provided more security. Until they found the murderer, no one on the moon was safe.

Counselor Contor came in to the Comm room.

"Good morning, Counselor," Berto said.

"Good morning. Have you seen Commander Howell?"

"Not this morning, sir. Usually no one comes in here unless they are passing through, or they have a message to send," he said.

"I see."

"Sir? Can I ask you a question?"

"Of course."

"We've been hearing talk that a change in the edict for taking mates of another race may be up for a vote when the Council of Nations meets later this month. Is that so?"

"Yes, Berto. I'm trying to get people to discuss a change in the edict now."

"May I say something, sir?"

"Go ahead. I'm always interested in hearing what my constituents have to say."

"I worked for the criminal, Dram, until recently. Dram was in the slave trading business, as you may know."

"I'm familiar with his crimes. That is why I'm pushing for this change in the edict."

"Yes, sir. Some of the slaves were bought for procreation. There were complete villages destroyed by his actions. If you punish the few people that this affects by exiling them to Plumaris, which is inhabited by criminals, you essentially are eliminating the races that Dram affected. If they are allowed to live in their own home villages, they would be more productive there than they would be on Plumaris."

"I agree. You see, Berto, the village I belonged to on Tarsius was attacked by his men when you were much younger. They took my sister and a group of female students from the academy. I am prepared to accept my sister back into what is left of our family when she is found. I couldn't bear to know that she would be lost forever, exiled on Plumaris because...because of what happened to her."

"Well, sir, I'm from Tarsius, too, and if you need my support, you've got it. Some of the recruits agree that we need a change. Besides, you can't predict who you will fall in love with." He remembered how he felt when he first saw Shey.

"Berto, I'm afraid the most difficult task for the recovered slaves will be assimilating back into the societies they were taken from. Those that have been gone the longest may not want to leave their present home. Each situation will have to be dealt with separately," the Counselor said.

Howell stepped into the communications room. "Berto, we'll meet in my office in ten minutes. Agent Texler will take your shift for the meeting."

"Yes, sir."

"Howell, a word with you, please?" the Counselor asked. The two left the room and in minutes, Texler showed up.

He checked his chrono. "Right on time, Texler." He exited the room and headed for Howell's office.

He sat in the back of the classroom, where he had been ushered by an agent he didn't know. The officers of Meta Station, including Shey, sat up front, while a few I.S.P.

agents and dignitaries sat behind them. The room was packed. Howell addressed the group.

"Commander Hammon will speak to you on the findings of the investigation," Howell said, then sat down.

"Gentlemen," he coughed. "Excuse me, Officer Shey and everyone else, we have done a thorough investigation on the body of Agent Jans and have found that he had been poisoned."

"What?" Someone called out.

"Jans' stomach contents were full of the same food everyone else had eaten. However, the food source itself was not tainted. The contents of his stomach contained two chemicals which are harmless alone, but when combined, are deadly. One is generally found in liquid form, the other in plant form."

"Do you have any suspects?" Howell asked.

"As of now, we've narrowed down our findings to one of four people," the Commander said, "Cower, Tabon, Shey, and Tam."

Shey? The room broke out in loud talking.

Berto stood up. "Did you look at the vids, sir?"

Howell turned around. "What vids?"

Lander leaned next to Howell and whispered something.

Howell stood up and spoke to Commander Hammon.

"It looks like this investigation is not quite over. We'll meet again here in the morning," Hammon said.

The room quickly cleared out with Howell and Hammon leaving first, then Lander, Derek, Bover, Cower...

He stood in the back corner, watching for Shey. How could they come to that conclusion? He couldn't see Shey poisoning Jans. Then his heart skipped a beat. She brought the food for him, not Jans.

15

After viewing the vids, Hammon looked at his comm-pad and tapped it. He scrolled down with his finger. "Tam has an alibi. She said she was at the lounge all night."

"And she has witnesses to that fact?" Shey asked.

"Yes, she does," Hammon said.

"What about when she handed me the plate here in the Comm room? Davmic saw her."

"I'll check with Davmic on that. You, however, don't have any witnesses to corroborate your story that you were in your room all night."

"I worked on assignments. That information should be on my comm-pad," Shey said.

"Plus, the person in the vid was taller than 6.5 centikiks, sir," Berto added.

"Play that vid again," Hammon ordered CO Derek.

Derek pulled it up for him and paused the frame.

"Cower and Tabon were in their quarters, I was with them," Lander said.

"Where did Tam get the food, then?" Berto asked.

"The plate was warm, so it had been heated recently," Shey added.

"Get Tam and Davmic in here, Commander," Hammon said to Howell. Howell spoke to Texler and Texler left the room.

"That still doesn't answer the question of who went into that ship," Berto said.

"I have the height and weight records of all the recruits," Shey added, "if you need them."

Texler came back into the room and spoke to Howell then Howell spoke to Hammon. Hammon tapped his communicator. "Agent Swilla, meet me in the Comm room at Meta Headquarters, and bring your team."

"Yes sir."

Within minutes, Agent Swilla and his team entered the Comm room from outside.

"Agent Swilla, I want you to conduct a thorough examination of the recruits' quarters while they're in PT. Use any scanners you deem necessary. I want nothing overlooked, no matter how innocent it appears."

"Yes sir."

Howell ordered CO Derek to call all the recruits to the PT field.

"Will that be all, sir?" Berto asked Howell.

"Yes, for now, Berto."

When the group of recruits filed out the door, Berto followed, with Shey behind him.

Danner rushed out the door with them. "This would be a great time to incorporate our two lessons on opportunities," Danner said to Shey.

"Yes, it would," she agreed.

Tam stood in Howell's office along with Davmic.

"Why are we here?" she asked Zendra.

"The Commander has a few questions he'd like to ask each of you," the agent said.

"We've already answered the questions," she said. "Or didn't he get the holo?"

"Your sarcasm is duly noted," Zendra said, making a notation on his comm-pad.

She rolled her eyes. *Easy, girl. You don't want to give anything away. You're too close to your goal to lose sight now.*

Davmic was called to the classroom first. She watched Zendra observing her behavior. She sat back in her seat with her hands behind her head. She could play the game. She had plenty of practice.

After fifteen minutes, Davmic came out and she was called in. She stood up and stretched then followed Zendra into the classroom. Calm and deliberate, she reminded herself.

"Have a seat," Commander Hammon ordered.

"Sure."

He cocked his head. "What is your problem?" he asked her.

"No problem."

"It seems we have a discrepancy in stories here."

"Oh?"

"Yes. It appears you were seen and heard talking to PT Officer Shey in the Comm room last night."

"How could I be in two places at once?" she asked.

"That's what I'd like to know. Who lied for you?"

She swallowed hard. "I don't know what you're talking about."

"Well, if you were in the lounge all night, except for

using the cleansing room, who do you have to back up that story?"

"Well, I can assure you that I am fully capable of using the cleansing room on my own. I have no witnesses to say they saw me in the cleansing room since all the other recruits are men, and I used my own cleansing room, in my quarters."

"How long were you gone from the lounge?"

"Just a few minutes."

"How many minutes?"

"However long it took me to relieve myself. Do you time yourself when you use the cleansing room?"

"I'll ask the questions here," Commander Hammon said. "Where did you get the food you gave to PT Officer Shey?"

"What food? What are you talking about?"

"Do you know what tannic is?"

"Hmmm. I don't think I've ever heard of it. What is it?"

"It's a plant that can be eaten raw or cooked. It looks like krinnage, but has a sweeter taste, and is found on Tarsius," the Commander said.

"Well, we aren't on Tarsius, are we?" she asked.

"Have you heard of cinesra?" Hammon asked.

"Hmmm, I think that's something you drink, right?"

"Yes. It is used for head pains," Hammon said.

"Well?" Tam asked.

"Well, what?" Hammon asked her.

"Why do you want to know if I know what they are?"

"It shows in your record that you worked for a healer back on Tarsius, is that true?"

"For a short time, yes."

"What did you do afterward?"

"I came here."

"You don't remember using cinesra or tannic while working for this healer?"

"I didn't use them, but that doesn't mean the healer didn't use those things," she said. *Of course the healer used them, wombit.*

"Have you ever had head pains?"

"I can't say that I have." But Hammon was sure giving her one now. She was bored with his questions. "Look, what is this leading up to?"

"I said, I'll ask the questions around here."

She rolled her eyes. This had to be calm and deliberate. If she wavered they would know.

"Who gave you the food you gave to Shey?"

"What are you talking about? I didn't give food to anyone."

"Did you find a plate of food in the food prep room the other day?"

"I didn't go into the food prep room. I'm a recruit. We aren't allowed in there."

The Commander tapped his communicator. "Agent Zendra, please escort Recruit Tam to solitary."

"What?" She stood, hands on hips. "On what grounds?"

"You are a belligerent prevaricator, Tam. I will question you again when I'm finished here," Hammon said.

Agent Zendra stepped inside with a laser rifle pointed at her. "This way," he said.

She clenched her teeth. *Be calm. Be deliberate.* She lifted her chin and let Zendra lead her to solitary on the Escort ship.

She would rather be in lockdown in the comfort of her own room, even if for a little while. This place was stark with its padded walls. The small cubicle had no windows, just a single door with two openings. The one on the bottom was for passing food trays. The second one higher up was for observation.

She could play this game of waiting. She sat down in the center of the room and crossed her legs. She began her slow, rhythmic breathing and the ancient chant that would help calm her.

There was a lot about her that no one knew, and no one would ever find out. Prevarication was a practiced art.

Howell stood in the Comm room when the class filed through the door. Berto walked up to him. "Excuse me, sir, but did you want me to finish working on the ships?" he asked.

"Yes, Berto, by all means. I'll get you clearance in just a minute. Each ship has its own guard now," Howell said. "CO Derek, can you get Berto clearance to work on the ships?"

"Yes, sir," Derek typed something onto the keypad. Seconds later, a badge popped out of the processor. He handed the photo ID badge to him. He glanced at the image. A recent one, taken when he surrendered himself to the I.S.P. Not bad for someone who looked as if he had second thoughts on what he was about to do. He pinned the badge onto his unicrin and headed out the door, while Derek notified the I.S.P. security.

When he reached the first ship, he re-checked everything he had done the night before. Once he was sure everything was all right, he powered up the systems and checked everything again.

He stepped out on the ramp and notified the guard, who in turn, notified Derek that the ship was test-ready.

After a few minutes, Howell came up the ramp.

"I'm looking forward to flying her, Berto."

"Me too, sir."

Howell did the pre-flight, while he awaited orders.

"All systems go," Howell said when he finished.

Take off was smooth. Howell took the ship through her paces. "She handles well, Berto."

"Yeah, real smooth, sir. I installed a power converter on this one. Dram used them to outrun the I.S.P."

"Well done, Berto, let's try it out."

He showed Howell the switches to use. Seconds later, they shot across the clear blue sky of Meta at super speed. "That will come in handy in a chase situation," Howell said.

"You have no idea, sir. Commander?" he asked.

"Yes, Berto?" Howell banked hard left away from the Nicca Valley.

"When I searched for Jans, I wasn't able to get into the second and third ships with the remote I had. My remote only worked on the first and fourth ship. Did you ever find Jans' remote?"

Howell's gaze jerked in his direction. "We never found that remote."

"Well, then, we still have a problem," he said.

"Re-wiring the entrance is time-consuming," Howell said.

"Yes, sir, but changing the codes and bypass switches is not."

"You can do that?"

"One of my specialties," he beamed. "That's how we jacked...uh, took those ships that Dram had." He swallowed his confession.

"Get on it when we get back."

"Commander, how is the investigation coming along?"

"Hammon determined that Cower and Tabon are innocent. Although they prepared the salad with tannic, there was no trace of cinesra anywhere in food prep. Someone with knowledge of poisons or chemical compounds would be more likely the guilty party," Howell said.

"They use tannic quite often in their salads and cooking," he said. "Besides, it grows wild around the three ponds."

"That's what the cooks told me, too," Howell said.

"So, who does Commander Hammon think is guilty?"

"Tam is being held for further questioning because she has discrepancies in her story, but she doesn't have a motive for killing Jans."

"What if it wasn't Jans she was after?"

"What do you mean?"

"Shey said Tam was bringing the food to me when she took the food from her. Maybe Tam and whoever worked with her didn't know Jans would be guarding the ship. Maybe they thought that was me in the third ship?"

Howell glanced at him as he banked over the Rift mountains. "That's right. Shey wasn't the only one with revenge issues against you. Didn't you have a problem with Tibu?"

"Yes, Tibu was extremely mad when I announced I had been working for Dram."

"I'll have the Commander take another look at this information," Howell said. He flew low into the landing area and reversed thrusters to set the ship down on the pad.

"I'll have names for the ships tomorrow," Howell said.

"And I'll have your new codes later today."

16

Berto worked on bypassing the switches and reconfiguring the codes on each ship to create new access codes for the hatchways.

"Wow, that was fast," Howell said when he turned them in.

"I had to be fast to get in the ship and steal it before anyone could catch me."

"I knew your skills would come in handy," Howell said.

"Thank you, sir. Oh, when I start working on the other ships tomorrow, I may need help with the wiring."

He headed out of the Comm room to find Danner and Semm to get his assignments. He checked his chrono. Danner was finishing up his class. He waited a few minutes in the eating hall to avoid Tibu before heading out. When he did, he found Danner in the hall.

"LEO Danner!"

Danner turned around. "There you are. I've got your assignments for the week."

He powered up his comm-pad and downloaded the lessons from Danner's larger pad.

"I'll need those by the end of the week, Berto."

"Sure." He hoped he had enough time to get everything done. Maybe he could work on the assignments when he pulled a shift in Communications tonight. "Have you seen Semm?"

"His class is next. We finished five minutes early."

Great. The class would be returning then as well. He headed to his quarters instead. Besides the four guards on the ships, they now had Zander watching the halls during the day. He passed Zander on his way to his quarters and nodded. His quarters-mates were inside taking a break.

"You've been making yourself scarce today," Telik said.

"Not on purpose. After our PT class this morning, I got one of the ships up and running. Howell took it out for a test. She flies real smooth." He gestured with his arm.

"I can't wait to fly one," Telik said.

"Did you find out who sabotaged the ship the last time you took her out?" Coz asked.

"No."

"So what's the news on the investigation?" Sags asked.

"Hammon is supposed to announce his findings in the morning. Have any of you heard anything?"

"I heard talk," Sags said. All heads turned toward Sags.

"Tibu and Tam have been hanging together until lately," he began. "I heard one of them talking about revenge. It sounded like Tibu. He and Tam worked out in the fitness room when no one was there. The door hissed open when I stopped to tie my boot strap in the hallway. They quit talking when they saw me get up."

"Did you hear anything specific?" Coz asked.

"No, just something like, 'I'll get even, wait and see'," Sags said.

"You know, after you called Tibu out on revenge in the lounge, he grumbled under his breath," Coz said.

He thought about that night and what had happened between him and Shey. Things were different between them now.

"I can't wait until lockdown is over," Telik said.

"Yeah, when are you coming back, Berto?" Sags asked.

"I'm here now. Howell has me working Jans' shift in communications."

"Are you still getting assignments from the instructors?" Telik asked.

"Yes, all but Shey. I'll be working on the other ships in the afternoons. I won't have time for the second PT class, at least, not now." He glanced at his chrono. "Class just started."

"Semm loves to give extra work if you're late," Telik said, grabbing his comm-pad and rushing out the door. Coz and Sags hurried after him.

He sat on his bed and worked on Danner's assignments. One of the lessons required him to search the LEWL and write up what he found on a name Danner gave him, so he did. But afterward, he had an idea. He typed in Tibu's name and waited. Nothing came up, so he tried Tam's name. Nothing. He searched the Chroma news databases and pulled up news vids, then searched under Tibu's name again. There was Tibu's name and image in the Brevin Chronicles. Recently graduated from the Brevin Academy of Sciences, Tibu ne Mar excelled in chemistry, the article read.

He copied the information into a folder on his comm-pad then searched for news vids from Tarsius. He scrolled down to Denoy and typed in the date fourteen anos ago. Nothing came up, except the incident involving the three boys who attacked his sister. The rush of energy at that memory stunned him. He took deep, calming breaths to control his anger. He never experienced his full power. What he had used that day to kill Mendo and Kalen was uncontrolled rage.

He searched for the Torren sector of Tarsius then typed in Mendo de Che's name. News vids popped up on the screen. He was bad from the start, like Kalen. There were some news vids about Che. He was bad, too.

He glanced at his chrono. Almost time to catch HCO Semm. He quickly saved his assignment and headed out the door with his comm-pad.

Before he reached the classroom, he noticed Agent Zendra with other agents by Howell's office. They escorted Tibu, Crocker, Dayton, and Kar through the eating hall. Kar and Tibu tucked their heads going through the doorframe. His quarters-mates came out seconds later.

"What's going on?"

"While we were in PT this morning, our rooms were searched," Telik said.

He remembered Commander Hammon's order.

"Apparently, something was found in their quarters," Sags added.

Just then, Bover rushed by, heading for the eating hall, carrying his comm-pad. While he watched Bover, he realized one of the two windows in the eating hall faced the pond area. He walked toward it. He remembered that sometimes Dram would stare out that window, gazing at the pond, no doubt remembering something. But what he hadn't realized was that he could see the ship on the first landing pad as well. Tibu must have seen him go up the ramp. He could easily slip out the back entrance, walk around the building, and hide behind one of the ships until Jans made his rounds, thinking it was him, instead. When

Jans went up the ramp, Tibu followed. The second landing pad could not be seen from this angle.

He swung around, intending to tell Howell, but found his quarters-mates staring at him. "I just realized what happened to Jans."

"Tell us!" Telik insisted.

"Tibu poisoned Jans, thinking it was me."

Coz' mouth dropped open. "How?"

"I'm not sure, but Tibu has knowledge of chemistry. He had no quarrel with Jans, but he did with me."

"So you think he took his revenge?" Sags asked.

"Yes! He must have known about the tannic in the salad."

"What are you talking about?" Coz asked.

"Tannic and cinesra are harmless by themselves but mixed together, they are deadly."

"Maybe you should share that information with Howell," Telik suggested.

"Howell knows."

"I'm talking about Tibu's knowledge of science and his motives toward you," Telik said, pointing at Berto.

Berto caught up with Semm as he walked through the eating hall doors. Inside, Crocker sat at a table on one end of the hall, speaking to two agents. At the other end, Dayton and Kar sat waiting, while two agents stood on alert. He followed Semm into the Comm room, where Commanders Howell and Hammon stood questioning Tibu, who sat in a chair against the wall. Davmic had the communications shift.

"This doesn't involve you, Berto," Hammon said.

Semm turned around, a surprised look on his face.

"I think it does, sir."

Hammon furrowed his brows.

"You see, Tibu killed Jans, thinking it was me."

"What?" Hammon demanded.

Tibu's eyes widened.

"Tibu has knowledge of chemicals, sir. He watched me go into the first ship then slipped out of the building. Waiting behind the other ships, he saw someone go up the ramps, thinking it was me, when it was Jans all along. He followed Jans into the ship and killed him."

Agent Swilla handed some items to Hammon.

"How do you explain these?" He opened his palms, one held a small stunner and an injector, the other a bottle of cinesra.

"I have head pains occasionally." Tibu glanced at the items.

"And what were you doing with a stunner?" Howell demanded.

Tibu hung his head.

"Take him to solitary and bring me Tam," Hammon told Swilla.

"Yes sir."

Swilla clamped restraints on Tibu.

Tibu jerked away and leaned toward Berto. "It should have been you that was poisoned!"

He took a deep breath, letting it out slowly, while Bover showed Hammon and Howell his background checks on the recruits.

Several long minutes later, Shey came into the room from the eating hall entrance, while Swilla escorted Tam from the outside entrance.

"Well, isn't this a nice little party?" Tam said, slowly glancing around the room.

"I'm going to ask you one more time, Tam, where did you get the food you gave to Shey?" Hammon demanded.

Davmic sat at the Comm board, his arms crossed, glaring at Tam. Shey crossed her arms, daring Tam to lie.

Tam winked at Berto, then smirked at Shey. "It was my food from the evening meal. I was hoping to get lucky with Berto that night, but Shey came along and spoiled my fun."

Shey's eyes widened at that confession, while Berto cleared his throat.

"Why did you lie about the food?" Hammon demanded.

"Well, according to regulations, recruits aren't supposed to fraternize with officers or other recruits, sir."

"I suggest you put her on probation, Commander Howell. Any more incidents of prevarication from her and she's gone," Hammon said.

"I'll take your suggestion under advisement, Commander," Howell said. "FI Bover, will you escort Tam to her quarters, please? She'll remain on lockdown except for classes for the remainder of the week."

"Yes sir. Tam?"

Tam walked out with Bover, kissing the air when she passed by Berto.

After their departure, Berto spoke up. "Sir, I have some information about the break ins of the fitness room."

"What is it, Berto?"

"Sags saw Tam and Tibu working out alone in the fitness room. I think they were behind the sabotaged equipment and unlocked door."

"I owe you an apology, Berto," Shey said.

He glanced at her. "Apology accepted, Shey, and I forgive you." If only she could do the same for him.

.   .   .

Tam let Bover escort her to her quarters. She faced him before he locked her inside. "I don't suppose you have any assignments for me to do while I'm in here, do you?"

"All your assignments from me are on the simulators. If HCO Semm or LEO Danner have something for you to do, I'll send them along. Otherwise, be prepared for a lot of work tomorrow."

Bover punched the button on the door panel and it hissed closed. After a few clicks, the door was locked from the outside.

Tam reached inside her boot and pulled out a small tool. She smiled as she studied it. *Yes, these locks are useless as long as I have you.* She kissed the tool and tucked it back inside her boot.

17

Berto shoved the wire and tools he needed for the second ship through the hatchway, when he heard one of Commander Hammon's agents speak to someone.

"What is your business here?"

He turned around.

"I'm PT Officer Shey. I came to get Berto. Commander Howell has an important announcement for all of us here at Meta Station," she said.

"She's okay. I'll go with her." Berto locked the ship with the ship's scanner, and slipped the strap over his shoulder. He took a few steps and stopped. "Where's your escort?"

"Howell is trusting me to come right back."

"Well, we better not keep him waiting, then."

He took longer strides than usual, but she kept up the pace. When they entered through the Communications room, Davmic pointed to his chrono.

"I have watch tonight. Will this take long?" Berto asked.

"I don't know. Howell's asked everyone to meet in the eating hall."

"I'll be back as soon as I can, Davmic." There wasn't enough time in the day anymore. He hadn't slept since the last watch. He and Shey entered the eating hall. The room was packed with Meta Station personnel as well as some of Hammon's people.

Commander Howell cleared his throat. "You will be glad to know that we have indeed finished the investigation. Things should be back to normal in the morning for most of you. However, there is one who will not be returning, so adjustments will be made. This afternoon, we got a confession from Tibu stating that he injected Jans with cinesra thereby causing the poison in his system. He did this as revenge against Berto, not realizing it was Jans."

"What happens to Tibu now?" someone asked.

"Murderers spend a lifetime on Plumaris. For those of you who don't know, Plumaris is a penal colony, mined for the precious metals and gases that are found there. Life on Plumaris is hard labor under heavy guard.

"Commander Hammon has graciously assigned Agent Zendra to assist us in communications until we finish with our training."

Bover stood up. "Berto has finished repairing one of the ships, so we will begin flight training in the morning. I have a schedule posted outside the classroom, so be sure to check which team you are on."

Then Shey stepped forward. "And the teams will have a little competition in PT to see who chooses the first ship."

He had forgotten about the teams. Once the teams were on their missions, he wouldn't see Shey anymore.

"I expect everyone to give it their best shot," Howell said. "Now that announcements are over you may all eat your evening meal."

He stepped through the door leading to communications. Davmic spoke to Zendra.

"Am I on watch, or has that changed?" Berto asked.

"If you take the first four, I'll take the second four, since neither of us has had any sleep today. Tomorrow night I'll be on full time," Zendra said.

"Great idea. Let me grab some food and I'll be right back." Berto said.

Berto slipped out the communications door and around through the food prep entrance.

"Hey, what did I tell you about coming through here?" Tabon said.

"There's no room in the eating hall," Berto said, "and I have to report to Communications."

Tabon handed him a plate. "Now get out of my food prep room."

"Thanks, Tabon." Berto rushed out the food prep door before Tabon changed his mind and re-entered through communications. He shoveled the food down, while Davmic filled him in on what was going on.

Davmic took Berto's plate when he left. Everything quieted down for a few minutes. Then, just as suddenly, Commander Hammon burst through the door with his agents following behind.

Howell and some others came in shortly after and the noise level grew. Within minutes, Howell walked them back to the Escort ship.

"I think I liked it better when it was quiet," he said aloud.

"I always thought you were the quiet type," Shey said.

He swung around in his seat. "When did you slip in?"

"I came in with Howell. It's been noisy around here with Hammon's people." She clutched her comm-pad to her chest and remained on the far side of the room. She played it safe. He couldn't blame her.

He realized they hadn't been alone together in awhile.

"No supervisor tonight?"

She shook her head. "I'm waiting for Howell."

Shey looked like fresh flowers in her pink tunic. The color suited her. He wanted to kiss her so bad it hurt, but he couldn't handle the heartache any more. It was a dull pain now. Eventually it would go away. At least, that's what he kept telling himself.

"Howell told me that the Commander and his crew will be leaving at first light," Shey said.

"Maybe things will get back to normal, then," he said.

"What about us?" Shey asked.

He hesitated, hanging his head. "We've been over this, remember? Until you can forgive me, there is no us." And the mere words caused a heaviness in his heart, just the same.

Shey chewed her bottom lip.

Howell returned. "I'm sorry to keep you waiting, Shey. Let's go to my office."

"I've set up the teams for a reason, Shey. I know you have issues with Berto, so I took that into consideration. But I had to put you and Tam together because of sleeping arrangements."

"Yes, sir." It made sense, but she didn't have to like it.

"The teams have more to do with flight experience and leadership qualities than anything else. FI Bover and LEO Danner gave me their recommendations. Since you are still an officer in training, I paired you with LEO Danner. He has more field experience, where the others have more class experience."

"I understand, sir."

"PT Officer Shey, give him a second chance." Howell reached out and touched her arm.

She nodded. What else could she do? They would be team mates whether she approved or not. As an officer, she couldn't hold a person's background against them.

"I want you to keep an eye on Tam for me. There's something about her that just sets off my alarms, but I can't put my finger on it."

She felt the same way about Tam. "I know what you mean, sir."

"Good."

She stood to leave.

"One other thing, Shey."

"Yes, sir?"

"Berto may need some help pulling wires on the other ships. If you have time, could you help him with that?"

"What about my supervisory stipulation around students?"

"I put that stipulation on you because of something Tibu and Tam had reported. I figured they were just trying to start something." He hesitated. "Are you feeling vengeful around him?"

She lowered her head. "No sir, not anymore."

"Well, if you can behave like an officer around him, then I trust you."

And if I can't? "Yes sir."

Tam sat on her bed with her comm-pad, catching up on assignments.

When they let her out for evening meal, she'd learn her team assignment. If Berto wasn't on her team, she would have to act quickly since there were only three weeks left in class.

Four hours later, Zendra showed up in the communications room. Berto glanced at his chrono. "Right on time." Berto stood up and stretched.

After filling in Zendra, he stopped by the classroom to see what team he was on. He rubbed his eyes and looked again. Danner's team? He was okay with that, but Shey's name was listed beneath Danner's, then his, Coz, and Tam. His heart pounded. Being with Shey on a small ship was just pure torture.

He headed to his quarters for a full four hours of sleep.

"I can't wait."

18

———

After PT and the morning meal, Berto headed for the landing pad where the second ship sat. It was strange not seeing the extra guards. And just as Shey had said, Commander Hammon's ship was gone, too.

He took the scanner and went through the ship to see what needed repairing. He assessed the materials he had and went to storage to retrieve more tools and parts. On his way back, he saw Lander working on the first ship, painting the name Spurius over the hatchway.

"I thought FI Bover was taking her out today," he said.

"Oh, he is. He wanted a name on it before they headed out."

"Will it dry in time?"

"Yes. This is special paint. It dries in minutes."

"Are you painting all the others today, too?"

"Yes. You're working on the Pandarus right now."

"Well, I guess I better get started then."

. . .

It seemed like minutes, but when he glanced at his chrono, a few hours had passed when he heard a voice.

"Berto?"

Shey?

He climbed up from the engine room and into midships before stumbling out the hatchway. He was glad to see her, but he wasn't sure why she was here.

"Commander Howell said you needed help with the wiring," she said, coming up the ramp.

"I did...I do...need help. Yes." He was so glad to see her he couldn't think straight.

She cocked her head. "Are you sure? Because I can work on assignments if you don't need my help."

"No! I mean...yes, I'm sure...I do need help."

She followed him into the ship and down the steps to the engine room.

He had to control himself. Why was he feeling nervous? He had been alone with her before.

"It's the same thing we did the other day, except I had already started it by myself."

"I see." The wires lay jumbled in a mess. Shey bent to help him straighten the wires then feed them through the pipes.

He climbed up the steps and grabbed the ends, weaving them into the Nav room pipes.

"This is so much easier with your help, Shey."

Another couple hours passed while he and Shey worked on the Nav-u-com, connecting all the loose ends, until his stomach growled.

She glanced at her chrono. "You know, we can stop to eat and finish this later."

"Yes. Good idea." He crawled out from underneath the panel then helped her up.

Berto followed the same routine every day for the next couple of weeks—PT, morning meal, then working on the ships. Shey showed up after her second PT class and helped until noon meal. Then he worked alone until evening meal, finishing his assignments before going to sleep.

Shey was professional toward him, like an officer should be. There were times when she shared some of her childhood and adult memories. He even mentioned a few of his own. He felt closer to her now and looked forward to their time together. There was a chance that happiness had not completely eluded him. He wanted more, though. He wanted the love that usually went with a mated couple. Did he deserve it? No, not after the life he led, but he wanted it.

By the end of the second week, he had finished the last ship. Howell came up the ramp as he secured the ship.

"Hello Commander. I was just locking up."

"Mind if I take a look?"

"It's your ship, sir." He ushered Howell in with an arm gesture.

"I don't know how we could have done this without you, Berto. Central command didn't budget for extra personnel to repair these ships."

"How did they get them here in the first place?"

"A military class A destroyer brought them here from Tarsius Station. They used a small tug to tow them to this moon. Next week was when they planned to send someone to work on the ships. One week to do the work it took you three weeks to do." Howell shook his head. "I don't think they realized the extent of repairs needed."

"Uh, yeah, and they never would have gotten the power converters installed either."

"That was a nice touch, Berto." He patted him on the back. "Is the Eligius ready for her test run?"

"Yes sir."

"Let's do it, then."

The Eligius was the ship Jans died in. It had three sleeping compartments, where the others had only two, which made it a little larger. This was to be his new home, at least on missions.

"Sir, there's something I have to tell you," he began, after he and Howell strapped in.

"What is it, Berto?"

"I found Dram's program modifier in storage and downloaded the new I.S.P. enhancements from Hammon's ship onto the modifier."

"He let you do that?"

"Well, he's not missing anything, sir. I just copied files onto the program modifier and then uploaded them to our ships. I tested everything before we ran our test flights, so I know everything works."

"So how will that affect our ships?"

"To everyone looking at these ships, they look like they belong in a recycler for spare parts."

"But?"

"These ships think and respond like military escorts. All we need are some big weapons."

Howell rubbed his chin and smiled. "I think I know where I can get those."

After the test flight, Berto locked up the Eligius. Only he and Howell had the codes to the ships.

Everyone moved about Meta Station with a little more

excitement and purpose, now that Bover had the class flying every day. He took three at a time for thirty minutes each. Everyone had to get their flight time in before he checked them off, himself included. Once the final ship was ready, Shey had the teams compete for the choice of ship.

Bover's team picked the Spurius, Semm's team picked the Aquilla, and Howell's team got the Pandarus. By default, Danner's team got the Eligius because they had an extra crew member and the ship was bigger.

"I think it was planned," he whispered to Sags.

"Our team beat everyone else," Sags said. "You're jealous."

"Not me! I'm on the biggest ship." He leaned back in his seat, his hands behind his head. "Besides, I have two beautiful women to look at every day. You have Crocker and Zed."

Sags waved him off.

Shey overhead Berto tease his quarters-mate about their ships. Berto thought they were both beautiful? He never said anything to her before.

She missed not working with him on the ships. He patiently showed her what to do, never scolding her when she did something wrong. He finished all the ships last week, and during that time, she did a lot of thinking.

She missed her brother Kalen. He had been kind to her, but something had been seriously wrong with him to treat girls the way he did. Maybe he hadn't tried anything with her because she had been scrawny and plain growing up. It wasn't until she turned seventeen anos that her body really filled out. But Kalen had been dead for ten anos by then.

Her father Kaal was right. It was time to let go of Kalen's

memory. It was time to live her own life and grab some happiness before she grew too old to experience it.

She cared for Berto. He was kind and patient and the way he loved her that night was incredible. She wanted more of his touch, but as a recruit she couldn't have him. It was all she could do to keep from touching him when they worked together. Did he still care for her?

This coming week was the final assessment of their studies. If she passed all her testing, she would be an officer. Berto, on the other hand, would be an agent.

Berto finished stowing gear, food and supplies for a trip in space. Afterward, he checked his list once more on his comm-pad to make sure he didn't forget anything. He looked up when he heard Howell board the ship.

"Are we ready for flight?" Howell asked.

"Yes, sir," Berto said, looking past Howell for any passengers.

"It'll just be the two of us this time," Howell said.

Berto and Howell strapped in, then went over another pre-flight check list.

"You've got some nice upgrades, here, Berto. Are these the upgrades you got from Commander Hammon's ship?"

"Yes, sir." Berto opened his palm and showed Howell a stick-disk.

"Where did you get that?"

"It's Dram's program modifier. I can plug this into any Nav-u-com and download information and software applications. Then, I plug it into a deficient Nav-u-com and upload it. Since the Commander had so many appliances and features on his ship, I thought we could take advantage of that information."

"Well, we aren't supposed to be that sophisticated yet, but I guess it wouldn't hurt to get a jump start," Howell said.

"This same device is how I upgraded all Dram's ships. His partner, Timna, showed me all I know," Berto said. He handed the device to Howell.

"Engage engines," Howell said. Within minutes, the ship was off. Howell flew her over the three ponds and decided to circumnavigate the moon.

"Sir, if you push this lever," Berto pointed at the instrument, "I'll get Davmic on the comm-link so he'll be ready to check our fly-by."

"We have plenty of time for that," Howell said.

Berto shook his head. "Trust me, sir, we won't."

Howell pushed the lever as Berto keyed the comm-link.

"Ready for fly-by in five...four...three...two...one—"

"Damn!" Davmic called out.

"How did we do?" Howell asked, keying the comm-link.

"Sir, I...I, it's faster than the speed-meter can read, sir," Davmic said.

"Over 300?" Howell asked.

"Mine goes to 500, sir, and it was faster than that," Davmic said.

Berto and Howell returned to Meta Station late that night, without Zendra picking them up on scanners.

"That's amazing, Berto," Howell said. "No wonder we could never catch Dram."

"Dram made sure we had state of the art equipment, if he had to steal it himself. Timna was a master at systems tech and taught me a lot. He's the one that modified those units I used for speed enhancement," Berto said.

"See you in the morning, Berto," Howell said.

It was late. Berto hesitated at Shey's door. He wanted so much to see her, but she had to begin the fitness competition in the morning. Just as he turned to leave, the door opened and Shey stuck her head out.

"Where do you think you're going?" Shey asked, grabbing Berto's arm.

Berto let her drag him into the room. He wrapped his arms around her and kissed her firmly on the lips. Within seconds, he was ravaging her mouth. He wanted her more each time he saw her.

"I missed you today," he said. It surprised him to admit it, but it was true. He had thought about her all day, and when Howell wouldn't let her and Danner come along for the ride, he was disappointed.

Shey kissed him deeply, then pulled him toward the bed. It didn't take much to convince him to stay.

Early the next morning, and tired from lack of sleep, Berto and Shey headed out toward the track after picking up some equipment from the fitness room.

"Today, I'm having different races along the track," Shey said. "Bover, Danner, and Semm will be here shortly to help me set things up."

"Will you need my help?" Berto asked.

"I can always use your company, but you don't need to do anything," Shey said.

After a short run, Berto left and got an early start on the ships. He had to install all the new weapons and cloaking devices he and Howell had picked up the day before from an old trading post on the outskirts of Tiga, another moon of Plexus. Apparently, Howell had arrested the owner of the trading post anos before. The owner was willing to trade information for a lighter sentence. If Howell trusted the man, it was fine with him. Berto managed to get all the cloaking devices installed before eating his morning meal. Afterward, he ran his systems checks before installing the weapons.

After the noon meal, Shey helped him install the smaller weapons on all the ships. She was a lot stronger than he thought, but the turbo cannons were too heavy for one person to hold up while installing the hardware to hold them in place.

"Tomorrow I'll get a couple of men to help me install the turbo cannons before I run the tests for all the new pieces." Berto said.

"Will you be finished with everything tomorrow, then?" Shey asked.

"If all goes well, I will."

The next day, as Berto approached the ramp of the Eligius, Tam stepped out of the ship and down the hatchway. The hairs on the back of his neck stood up.

"What were you doing in there?" he demanded.

"I was looking for you," Tam said.

"These ships are off limits to everyone," Berto said.

"Oh? Well, I just did my flight training on the Spurius last week and I wasn't told that," Tam said.

"Stay off these ships," Berto said, raising his voice. He

knew the codes were safe on the other ships, but how did she get on this one? Did he forget to lock up?

"Well, that's going to be hard since I was assigned to this ship," Tam said.

"What do you want?" Berto snapped. Tam wasn't getting the hint.

"I came to ask if you needed help with finishing the work on the ships," Tam said.

"Uh, no! I've got all the help I need, thank you." He glanced over his shoulder. Telik, Sags, and Coz came up behind him.

"Is everything all right?" Sags asked, crossing his arms over his chest.

"I was just offering my assistance," Tam said.

"I don't think you can help this time, Tam." Coz said, moving to the hatchway.

Tam walked down the ramp, gazing first at Berto then Sags, Coz and Telik as she passed them. "Your loss," Tam mumbled.

Berto watched to make sure she was gone before heading up the ramp with the hardware.

"What was she doing here?" Sags asked.

"That's a good question. I caught her coming out of the ship when I returned with this equipment. I must have left the ramp down." Just to be safe, he'll let Howell know about this situation.

"Let's do a systems check," Telik suggested.

"We will, but first let's get the weapons mounted."

The four of them went inside to the engine room. The turbo cannon was on the floor. Berto handed Coz the hardware and together they installed it in the weapons bay. Telik and Sags picked up the turbo cannon and set it in the cradle, with Coz and Berto guiding it in place. Berto fastened a compressor module onto the cradle so it could communicate with the Nav-u-com.

"How did you get the laser cannon installed by yourself?" Telik asked.

"I didn't. Shey helped me with that."

"Is that all you wanted us to do?" Sags asked.

"Well, we do have three more ships."

The four of them moved on to the other three ships and repeated the steps from the first installation.

When the last cannon was in place, Berto initiated the testing sequence.

"Sags, you take one cannon, Telik, you take the other," he said.

"Oh, this feels good," Sags said, moving his seat in all the positions. He took aim top, bottom, left and right.

"How about you, Telik?" Berto asked.

"This one is smooth. I like the way it handles," Telik said.

"Too bad you won't get to use it," Coz added.

"Why do you say that?" Telik asked.

"You've got pilot duty. You won't be in a position to shoot," Coz said.

"All right men, let's run the tests for the cloaking device. Everyone to the Nav-room."

They climbed the steps to mid-ships and headed for the Nav-room.

Once inside, Berto had Telik take pilot's position with Coz as co-pilot. He initiated the testing sequence for the cloaking device.

"Everything seems to be working," Telik said.

Sags stood in the back and watched.

"Power down," Berto said. "We're good here."

Berto, Sags, Telik and Coz moved on to the other ships, testing each one and taking turns.

Finally, they moved to the Eligius.

"I want to do a little more testing on this one," Berto said.

"Why is that?" Sags asked while sitting in the turbo cannon seat.

"Something about Tam makes my skin crawl." Berto initiated the testing sequence.

"Why?" Coz asked, sitting in the laser cannon seat.

"I don't know. I just can't get myself to trust her."

"After her and Tibu's scheming, I don't trust her either," Telik said.

"The investigation never uncovered who tampered with the ships, but the vids showed someone on the short side coming out of the ship," Berto said.

"Yes, and most of us are at least 6 centikiks except for one person," Telik said.

"Tam," Coz added.

"We're good here, then?" Sags asked.

"We're good. Let's head up to the Nav-room," Berto said.

Berto initiated the testing for the cloaking device and everything checked out. Then he ran the systems checks as well as pre-flight.

"Everything seems to be fine," Sags said.

"We're good, then?" Telik asked.

"It seems so, for now." Berto couldn't shake the feeling that something didn't feel right. He didn't get that feeling very often, but when he did, he couldn't let go of it because it usually proved to be right.

19

The next morning, everyone was outside on the track, ready to begin the commencement exercises. Counselor Contor was there. He congratulated everyone, announcing the ships' names and each flight team.

"Tomorrow, you will venture out on your first mission. Each team will go in different directions but you will all be working on the same goals: to find the slaves and return them to Tarsius at the I.S.P. Headquarters. While there, they will be debriefed before returning to their home planets," Contor said. "You may also be pleased to know that several members of the council have brought forth a bill to allow all residents of the Vaedra System to choose mates of their own, regardless of their race. And the mixed-race people can live, visit, and enjoy commerce anywhere in the Vaedra System without reprisals. All formerly exiled mixed-race people are forgiven and may return to the Vaedra System if they so choose. A vote will be forthcoming in the next month."

Cheers and whistles rang out at the news. Contor waved his arms until everyone quieted down. "Commander Howell tells me that evening meal will be at 1800 hours and there will be a social afterward."

More cheers rang out until Howell calmed everyone down. After the ceremony, Howell called each new agent by name and issued the standard white flight suit with matching jacket with the I.S.P. insignia on the front of both, a pair of black, lace-up, all-weather boots, a laser pistol with thigh holster, and a communicator that could be worn on the wrist or shoulder.

Evening could not come fast enough. He'd missed the first social when Shey danced with every man on the moon except him. Tonight, she would be his, if she would only forgive him.

Back in his quarters, he found some clean clothes to wear to the social. After cleaning up, he took a little extra time getting ready.

"Do you mind if I ask Shey to dance?" Coz asked Berto.

He glared at Coz. What nerve! Then he remembered she was one of two women. Of course everyone would want to dance with her. "Why ask me that question?"

"Hey, we all know you have a thing for her, but it's my last chance to dance with a woman before our mission."

He clenched his teeth. "Why do you think I have a 'thing' for her?"

"It's obvious."

So much for keeping his feelings to himself. "Only if you show me how to dance."

"You don't know how to dance?" Telik asked.

"I never learned."

"Here. Watch my feet." Coz made a few moves. "Try it."

He repeated what Coz did.

"Great. Now do this." Coz took a few steps and he repeated them.

"Now, put all that together."

Berto tried the first steps, then added the second steps.

"You got it! Now just keep doing that all night."

"That's it?"

"For a beginner, that's all you need," Telik added.

"What do I do with my hands?" he asked.

"Come here, Telik," Coz said.

"No way."

"We have to show him how to hold a woman."

"I think Berto can figure that out for himself."

Coz stepped too close to him, moving an arm behind his back and grabbing his hand.

"What are you doing?"

"This is how you hold a woman while dancing. Now try those moves."

He tried moving his feet while holding Coz's hand. It felt awkward, but his feet moved better than the rest of him.

"Just practice the footwork. Once you've got her in your arms, you look into her eyes and keep moving your feet," Coz explained.

"Yes. Don't look at your feet," Telik added.

He practiced the foot pattern until he could look up and do it without tripping.

Sags walked into the room from the cleansing unit. "What did I miss?"

"Dance lessons," Telik said, heading to the cleansing unit.

There was a knock on the door.

"What happens in this room, stays in this room," Berto said, pointing at both Sags and Coz.

Coz opened the door. "Commander Howell, come in."

"Sorry to interrupt your packing, men, but I thought I'd tell you we have a ship coming in with guests on it for this evening."

"Guests?" Berto asked.

"Yes, some of our new female recruits from our training facilities on Tarsius. They finish up their training next week. I worked out a little R&R with their leader. They had more female recruits than we had." Howell saluted and left.

"I guess we won't be fighting over Shey," Coz said.

A renewed excitement enveloped him. Maybe he would have Shey to himself after all. He continued practicing the dance steps as he packed his things.

A few hours later, all the new agents were called to their ships for loading and inspection. Each team leader was present to open the hatches and supervise the loading of gear, food, and supplies.

"Berto, you and Coz will bunk here." Danner pointed to the furthest sleeping quarters. "Shey and Tam will bunk in here." He pointed to the center quarters. "These are my quarters." He pointed to the one closest to the Nav-room. Everyone stood at attention outside their sleeping quarters.

Danner inspected the Eligius, marking things off with his comm-pad. Then Danner went below and inspected the weapons that Berto and his quarters-mates had installed. When everything checked out, Danner dismissed everyone.

The guests from Tan Station on Tarsius arrived. Introductions were made before the evening meal and room was made for them at the tables.

Shey sat with the other instructors, so he was stuck with his quarters-mates drooling over the new female guests. The four additional women would allow him some time to spend with Shey. At least, he hoped so. Their leader was a

Lieutenant Trayka from Vestra Major, and she had her eye on Howell.

A woman sat on either side of him. He was at a loss for words. He watched as Coz and Telik made small talk with them and he tried to follow along.

"I'm the systems tech for Tan Station," the beautiful Tarsian on his right said.

He choked on his food. "How long have you been there?" he managed to ask the brown-haired, brown-eyed woman.

"Two anos. I'm not training with the others. I get all the ships ready to fly."

"Berto's our systems tech," Coz interrupted.

"Really? Maybe we can exchange tips. My name is Reeva." She offered her hand.

He shook her hand but she was reluctant to let go. She leaned close. "I see you have an acquaintance of mine as a new agent."

"Who is that?" Berto asked.

"Tam," she whispered.

He pulled back. "How do you know her?"

"My sister is a healer and Tam apprenticed with her for a short while but she didn't have the gift. She started hanging with me, learning about systems. Is she a tech here as well?"

"No. I'm the only systems tech, although Shey had some experience with cruisers and now the class B wing ships."

"Shey?"

"She's my...part of my mission team." How could he describe her? His lover? His friend? The woman he wanted to spend a lifetime with?

"Shey's coming over," Coz whispered to him.

"Shey! This is Reeva." He stood. "She's a systems tech on Tan."

She smiled at Reeva. "Could I have a word with you, please?" she said firmly.

"Sure. Excuse me," he said to Reeva then followed Shey out into the hallway.

"You looked pretty interested in what she had to say," she said, crossing her arms over her chest.

He looked her over carefully. Other than being jealous, she looked stunning. "You look delicious," he said, licking his lips.

She clenched her jaw.

"What's wrong?"

"I heard that Reeva is quite a woman around Tan," she said.

"Really?"

"Yes. Word is, she keeps all the men around her...pleased."

"Well, I have you and she doesn't interest me in the least." He pulled her close and kissed her nose.

"That's not what it looked like from where I was sitting."

"It's what she told me that should interest you the most." He waggled his brow at her.

20

———

At 0500 hours, Meta time, all agents awoke and prepared for their first mission. By 0530 hours, everyone ate the last morning meal at Meta Station before final inspection. At 0600 hours, all teams lined up in front of their ships, awaiting Commander Howell's final orders.

"Good luck, everyone. When your mission is completed, you will return to Meta Station for further instructions. Your orders have been sent to your Officer's comm-pads. Dismissed."

"Well, crew, this is it. Everyone on board the Eligius," Danner said.

Once inside, Danner pulled up his orders on his device.

"It looks like we've all been promoted. From now on, I will be Law Enforcement Master Chief Danner. In public, you will call me Master Chief, but on this ship, you'll call me LE Danner. Is that clear?"

Everyone nodded.

"PTO Shey is PT1 Shey for Physical Training Officer, First Class. Berto is SMST Berto for Special Missions System Tech. Coz and Tam, you will both be SM Recruit for Special Missions Recruit. Is that clear?"

Everyone nodded and smiled.

"Our first mission is to Persus to recover the slaves sold to Taaka in the province of Izu. SM Recruit Coz, I want you to research Izu. I want to know everything about the climate, landing areas, the people and their customs. Report to me as soon as you find something."

"I'm on it, sir, uh, LE Danner." Coz said.

"SMST Berto, your assignment is to research Taaka. I want to know what kind of person he is and what kind of operation he runs."

"Yes sir, uh, LE Danner." He followed Coz to the food prep area where there was a pedestal table and benches. He pushed a button on the side of the table and two vid-screens popped up, back to back. Coz sat opposite him and tapped his comm-pad into one vid-screen. He did the same to the other. He pulled up Taaka on the LEWL database.

"SM Recruit Tam, you get to sleep because you will have second shift at the Nav-u-com."

"Yes, LE Danner, sir." Tam headed to her sleeping unit.

"I take it I have first shift?" Shey asked.

"Yes. Let's do a systems check before we get started," Danner said.

The mid-ship was empty except for Coz and Berto. Berto scrolled through the database. Taaka was a tribal leader in Izu. The tribe was large enough to cover a whole province. He tapped into the history data and discovered a disease wiped out most of their people over twenty-two anos ago. "Hmmm."

"What is it?" Coz asked.

"I think I understand why Taaka bought slaves from Dram. I'm going to tap into Meta's database while we're still here. I may get some information from Dram's reports."

"You can do that?"

"Yes. I helped de-code the information Ramen downloaded on a disc." He quickly used the passwords he had access to. "I'm in." He downloaded the info onto his commpad. "This may take awhile."

"Do you think it will help?"

"It can't hurt. I know Dram kept information on his contacts for future business transactions."

He typed in "Trade Partners". Nothing came up. He tried "Business Dealings", "Business Partners", and finally "Izu". With "Izu" he hit a large source of information.

"Here we go."

"What is it?" Coz came over to his side of the table.

All the information they needed was under the province name. Taaka met with Dram at a trading post near the Persus Station at Par Kava. The two struck a deal. Taaka needed men to work the fields and the mines. He paid in tulin, which was mined in Izu.

"Looks like they met again ten anos ago," he said. Reading on, it showed Taaka traded more tulin for women and girls. This time, it was for field workers and mates.

"Did Dram get these people from the same place?" Coz asked.

"No. It looks like the first group came from...Denoy." He looked at Coz. "My father could be in that group."

"Really? What about the second group? Where did Dram get the women?"

"Atria. That's where Genesis is from. She's a bounty hunter for the I.S.P. She mentioned her mother was abducted when she was young."

"How do you know this Genesis?" Coz asked.

"An Earthen I met talked me into helping him rescue her and some Chromian slaves on Vestra Minor. Shey was one of those slaves. Although I was part of the team that abducted them, I was also part of the team that rescued them."

"I don't understand. How could you be part of both teams?"

"The Earthen, Adam, is Dram's son. We were both training as Dram's pilots. Something went wrong with a delivery of slaves to Z on Vestra Minor so Dram sent us to rescue his crew. Adam had promised Genesis he would help her find her father but he wasn't good at navigation. He needed my help. That decision changed my life."

A soft pinging sounded. The signal to strap in for take-off. Coz returned to his seat and continued his research, while Berto pondered the possibility of seeing his father after all these anos.

Thirty minutes later, Shey came into the food prep area.

"SMST Berto, LE Danner wanted me to tell you that you have the second shift at the Nav-u-com." She sat beside him. "And SM Recruit Coz, if you have your report, he wants to hear it now."

"Sure." Coz untapped the comm-pad from the vid-screen and it lowered into the tabletop, then headed for the Nav-room.

"Did you have any luck with your research?" She gazed into his eyes.

He momentarily forgot what Danner had asked him to do. All he could think about were those pale blue eyes of hers and those tempting lips. He licked his lips just thinking about kissing her and the time he spent in her arms the night before. He leaned toward her, ever so close, without flinching.

"Yes," he said, his lips almost brushing against hers.

She reached her arm around his neck and pulled him into a full kiss. His arm reached around her waist, pulling her closer. His heart pounded in his chest. He wanted more of her. Instead, she pulled away.

"We...it will be difficult to remain on this ship without touching you," she said, breathless.

"Uh, yeah."

"When SM Recruit Coz is finished, LE Danner wants your report as well."

"I bet he does." He tried to pull away, but kissed her forehead instead.

"You will be working with Tam, you know."

"Don't remind me."

The door to the Nav-room hissed open. He untapped his comm-pad and returned the vid-screen to its original location and stood to meet with Danner. Shey remained at the table, waiting for Coz.

"You're up," Coz said in passing.

The Nav-room door hissed open at his approach.

"Hey SMST Berto, what have you got for me?" Danner asked, seeming more in his element here in space.

"How's she handling?"

"Oh, she's a beauty. Nice upgrades."

"I put a few extras in each ship, did Howell tell you?"

"Like what?"

"Like the modified hyper-drive and some software I picked up from Commander Hammon's ship."

He sat beside Danner and showed him some of the

features before sharing the information he gathered about Taaka and the dealings with Dram.

Afterward, he headed to his sleeping unit. Shey stood outside his door.

"Where's Coz?"

"I told him to get some sleep." Then she whispered, "He will be crewing for us." She kissed his cheek. "Sweet dreams."

He grabbed her up in his arms and kissed her passionately. Shey kissed him back, running her hands into his hair, pulling him closer. Her fingers brushed the knot in the back of his neck. "I'm sorry. Did that hurt?"

He pulled away slightly. "No, but now I won't get any sleep at all," he whispered as he stepped in front of the beam that opened the door.

Shey went back to the food prep area and fixed two hot beverages then headed back to the Nav-room. "Here you go," she said, handing one to Danner.

"Hey, you knew what I was thinking."

"So, did SM Recruit Coz and SMST Berto have any information for us?" Shey asked.

"Yes. I've already plotted a course for Izu. It's on the Vaedra side of the planet now, but I figure we'll arrive at night."

"Is that a good thing or a bad thing?"

"I would rather show up early morning with an element of surprise, than at night and not know where we are going. Most likely, we'll be on foot in the woods when we enter the village."

"So a night landing, then?"

"I think so."

"Will the five of us be able to take on a whole village?"

"I was assured there was another team on this mission along with a cargo transport team to pick up the slaves."

"Is that what you did in my rescue?"

"When we located you, we had scanners on top of the building to determine where to start our rescue efforts. Afterward, we dispatched teams for pickup. With this village, we'll use heat scanners, somewhat smaller than the scanners we used on Vestra Minor."

"We have heat scanners on board?"

"No. The cargo transport team will use those and report to us."

"How did you know where to find us on such a large planet?"

"Research, like SM Recruit Coz and SMST Berto did, helped a lot. Plus, we had Adam and Genesis who could communicate telepathically."

"That would come in handy on this mission," Shey said.

"Word is that Genesis' mother is among the slaves on Izu. She also has the gift of telepathy. I'm sure Genesis is part of one of the teams."

The thought of seeing Genesis again lightened her heart. Genesis had kept her from feeling despair at their situation.

"It'll be good to see her," she said.

"Yes. I only wish we could have talked Adam into joining the I.S.P. He would have been good at it."

"What happened to him?"

"As far as I know, he went back to Earth. The two of them together made a great team. I don't see how he could give all that up."

"I know she loved him." If Genesis and Adam didn't work out, how could she and Berto? Did she love Berto? Could she love him unconditionally after what he did?

"I saw them together. She did love him and told him so. I never heard him say it, but you could see it in his eyes." Danner said.

They sat in silence for a while. She thought of how she had treated Berto in the beginning, even though he had been only nice to her. She didn't deserve him.

"You know, Adam was the one who taught me those wrestling holds we used in class," Danner remarked.

"Really? They do that on Earth?"

"He learned it while studying at school."

Hours later, Berto came into the Nav-room.

"Care for a warm beverage?" He held two mugs out.

She stood and stretched, then reached for a mug.

"Thank you, SMST Berto."

He winked at her.

"Thanks. Are you and Tam ready to take over?" Danner asked.

"I am."

"I'm right here," Tam replied, standing behind Berto. She leaned against the entrance of the doorframe, her arms crossed over her chest.

Danner stood and stretched. "SMST Berto's in charge." He headed out the door.

Shey followed reluctantly. "See you in four." She winked.

"Strap in," Berto ordered as he sat down.

"You sure you know how to fly this thing?" Tam glared at him.

He glanced at her. "I've been flying for a couple anos. How about you?"

"You know I just learned. I didn't see you in flight training."

"That's because I already knew how to fly."

"How much longer to Persus?"

She annoyed him already. "Considering we were on the furthest moon from Vaedra and we're now headed for the closest habitable planet to Vaedra, I'd say a few days at this speed. Let's do a systems check."

"Why?"

He raised a brow at her. She obviously didn't pay attention in class. "How is it they passed you in your flight training?"

She sat with her arms crossed, pouting.

"I'd like to make sure everything runs smoothly during my watch. Is that all right with you?"

She didn't answer. He called out the different systems and she responded with the correct answer.

"See how easy that was?"

"Boring is more like it."

"Why don't you see if Coz can fix us something to eat," he suggested.

"I thought we had to have two people in the Nav-room at all times," she said.

"I think I'll be fine for two minutes."

"What did you want to eat?"

"Some soup would be good."

Tam left the room. She exhausted him. He grumbled at the thought of working with her the whole trip.

Tam headed for the food prep area. She hoped she wouldn't end up doing all the grunt work. That's all she ever did for her father when he wasn't serving time in some prison.

"Hmm." Coz wasn't here but his vid-screen was still up. She turned toward the engine compartment and opened the hatch. It was heavy. She managed to move it enough to slip down the steps. She located the comm wires and managed to cut one wire near the connection. It would be difficult to locate just one loose wire.

She quickly climbed back up the steps and slid the cover over the opening as Coz exited the cleansing compartment.

"What are you doing there?" Coz asked.

"SMST Berto wanted me to check something. He also wants you to fix soup for us."

She kept her hands hidden behind her back, trying to hide the wire cutting device up her sleeve.

"I'll bring the soup to you when it's finished."

"Great. Thanks." She walked inside the cleansing unit and took the cutting device out of her sleeve. She slipped the item into her boot and finished her business, then headed back to the Nav-room.

In the Nav-room, Tam sat down in her seat next to Berto.

"Is Coz fixing us a meal?"

"Yes. Soup," she mumbled.

After a few minutes, Coz brought them each a mug of soup.

"This is good, Coz. Did you take lessons in cooking?" he asked.

"Yeah, Tabon showed us a few tricks with space food one day. Tam was there," Coz said.

"You missed that class, too," Tam said. "In fact, you were hardly in any of the classes. What makes a criminal like you so special anyway? And why are you in charge?" she demanded.

He glared at her.

"What is your problem with Berto?" Coz asked. "What did he ever do to you?"

Tam turned away from both of them and looked out the viewport, crossing her arms, frowning.

Berto shook his head. "Coz, do you have any information on Izu's location?"

"Yes, it's in the north quadrant of Persus. I've uploaded the lat and lon to the Nav-u-com. I'm still working on the culture of the people."

He pulled up the coordinates and saw they were on course. Now he had a new problem with Tam. She definitely didn't like him. The feelings were mutual. He finished his soup and handed the mug to Coz. Coz picked up Tam's mug then left the room.

He pulled up his comm-pad and opened the files on Taaka, while Tam kept an eye on the horizon. After an hour, an alarm sounded.

"What's that?" Tam jumped in her seat.

He set his comm-pad down and moved his hands over the console, checking the system lights. He hit a switch. "We've got company," he said. Now that he was on the side of the good guys, who could it possibly be? His pulse kicked up a notch as a thought crossed his mind.

"What did you just do?" Tam asked.

"I switched on the cloaking descrambler."

"We didn't cover that in class." She glared at him.

"Yes, I know. It's one of my modifications. It unscrambles the sensors that cloak a ship so I can identify the ship that is approaching." A burning sensation started in his neck, then intensified.

"Damn!" He slapped the back of his neck. He felt a pulsing where the heat was emanating from.

Tam eyed him suspiciously. "What is it?"

"Hang on!" He moved the throttle forward and hit a couple of switches. Tam was thrown back in her seat. An intense gravity force held her in place like she was paralyzed.

"What are you doing?" She managed to ask.

"I put her into hyper-drive to escape the other ship."

"Why?"

"They were going to board us."

"How do you know that? I didn't see anything in the viewport."

"I told you they were using a cloaking device. That's why nothing was picked up on the sensors. Trust me on this. I know what I'm talking about."

"I've never heard of that," she said.

"Well, you wouldn't. You're just a new pilot. But you know a little something about systems, don't you?"

"What are you getting at?"

"You know what I'm talking about, Tam."

Tam clenched her jaw then turned away from him.

"We need to maintain the speed we're at so we can outrun them."

"Who are we running from?"

Berto glanced at Tam. He might as well tell her. Otherwise, she would keep asking these exhausting questions. Besides, they would all know soon enough.

Danner popped into the Nav-room. "I heard an alarm."

"You did," Berto said.

"We're being followed," Tam added.

Great. Her timing was impeccable. "I can't seem to shake them."

"What do you mean?" Danner asked, looking over the console.

"I put her into hyper-drive after my descrambler detected another ship trying to board us, but they managed to keep up with us," he said.

"Are you sure?"

"Yes. The alarm keeps going off when they get close," Tam added.

"Do you think they have a speed enhancer like we do?" Danner asked him.

"I'm sure of it."

"What's going on?" Shey entered the Nav-room.

He stood to let Danner take over a couple hours early. Why did this have to happen on *his* watch?

"We have company," Tam announced, standing so Shey could slip into the seat.

"You know that cargo transport Dram sent you on to Vestra Minor?" he asked Shey.

"The one that Dram stole from my father?"

"Yes, then blackmailed me for it."

Shey's eyes widened.

"Who paid you to steal it?" Danner asked.

"Pirates."

"But they didn't get the ship, Dram did," Shey added.

"You've endangered all of us!" Tam pointed at him.

"That's enough from you!" Shey stood and glared at Tam.

"What do they want?" Danner asked, adjusting the levers on the console.

"Me."

Three pair of eyes focused on Berto.

"How do they know you're on this ship?" Danner asked.

"Berto, your neck is glowing," Shey turned him around to inspect his neck.

"It burns, too. Something the pirates implanted on me and Bordon when we made the deal. It started pulsing the minute I turned on the descrambler."

"They've been tracking us because of you!" Tam shouted. "You brought them here, you fool."

"PT1 Shey, please escort SM Recruit Tam to her sleeping compartment," Danner said. "I won't have you talking about other members of this team like that." Danner pointed at her.

Shey took Tam by the arm and left the Nav-room.

"LE Danner, I'm sorry. I never thought they would find me. It's been four anos."

"How much do you owe them?" Danner asked.

"Bordon and I owe ten thousand credits each. I gave mine to my sister."

"Got any ideas?"

"You could cut the implant out of my neck, but they already know I'm here. We could destroy it once it's removed and then try to outrun them or change course."

Shey returned to the Nav-room. "I think we should lock Tam in the compartment, LE Danner. I don't trust her."

"Was Coz out there?"

"No, he's sleeping."

"Maybe I can rig something up to keep her in there," Berto said.

"We don't have time," Danner said. "We need to cut out that implant first."

"Cut?" Shey looked at Danner then Berto.

"Berto suggested it," Danner explained.

"Let me see that again," Shey rubbed her finger against the glowing skin. Just the slight touch of her finger excited him. "It doesn't look very deep."

Danner stood and looked over her shoulder.

"I could make an incision at this end and pull it out," she said.

"I don't know. It looks pretty risky with tendons so close," Danner said.

He turned and looked at both of them and saw the concern in Shey's eyes. "I trust you, Shey." He gave her arm a squeeze.

"Get Coz to help you," Danner said. "I'll keep things going here."

He and Shey went to Coz's compartment.

"You awake?" He knocked on Coz's door.

The door hissed open. "It's hard to sleep when you aren't tired and the alarm blares over your bed."

"Good. We need your assistance," Shey said.

Berto sat at the pedestal table in the food prep area. Shey injected him with a painkiller to numb the neck. Coz gathered towels and brought them to the table while she slowly removed Berto's flight suit from the shoulder area. She sanitized his neck. Taking a clean scalpel from the sanitized packet, she made a small incision.

"Here you go," Coz handed her a pair of sanitized tweezers.

She lifted the hair off Berto's neck with one hand and with the other, gently but firmly pulled the glowing object out from under his skin. She worked to stop the bleeding by applying pressure with a towel. Leaning close, she whispered in his ear, "Don't move."

Coz took the bloody object and handed her some bandages. Once the wrappings were in place, she cleaned Berto's skin with a wet cloth. Seeing his bare shoulders made her think about how firm those muscles were everywhere else. She missed touching his body and having her naked flesh against his.

"What do you suggest we do with this?" Coz held the object out for Berto to see.

Berto took the implant between fingers and crushed it like a trudge.

He reported to Danner when Shey finished her bandaging.

"How did you know of their approach?" Danner asked.

"I installed some upgrades like a cloaking device and a descrambler. That's why it took so long to finish the ships."

"Howell told me there were enhancements. I never expected this much," Danner said. "Call this in to warn the others."

He pressed the comm-link. "Eligius to Pandarus, come in."

No answer.

"Eligius to Pandarus, come in," he repeated.

No answer.

"Something's wrong."

Danner glanced at him. "Maybe we're too far out for them to pick up our signal."

"No, that was another upgrade I installed. This ship, along with all the others, was completed in Dram standards."

"What?"

"Dram had higher standards than the I.S.P. That's why he eluded you for so long. We can communicate with any of the other ships anywhere in this system."

"Try the others," Danner said.

"Eligius to Aquilla, come in."

"Are the pirates still out there?" Shey asked, entering the Nav-room with Coz.

"I've altered our course slightly," Danner said. "It should help us get away from the pirates."

Shey leaned over Danner's seat to check the console.

"Eligius to Spurius, come in," Berto said into the comm-link.

Coz stood behind Berto's seat. "Any response?"

"Nothing."

Suddenly the ship lurched forward, throwing Shey and Coz to the floor.

"What the Vaedran hell?" Danner shouted.

"They found us!" He jumped up from his seat to help Shey and Coz.

"Are you all right?" he asked Shey.

The ship lurched again and he pulled Shey into his arms as he fell back into the seat.

"Strap in!" Danner ordered. Coz took the safety seat behind the pilot and strapped in.

"This reminds me of when Z boarded our ship," Shey said.

He glanced at her and remembered he had tried to talk Adam out of rescuing Shey and the others. He was glad Adam won that argument.

Danner furiously tried to block the pirates from boarding, but it was useless.

"I have an idea," Berto said and motioned Shey to follow. The two of them left the Nav-room.

Tam stood outside her door, looking up at the boarding hatch. On her wrist was a glowing red ringlet.

Berto stood in the center of the open area and raised his arms. With his mind, he kept the hatch closed and forced the other ship off the Eligius. Within seconds, the ship lurched again. Tam and Shey fell to the floor. He concentrated on keeping the two ships apart.

"What is that on your wrist?" Shey demanded to Tam.

Tam glared at her. Shey reached for Tam's arm, but Tam pulled away and headed to her room.

"Shey, have Danner put the ship into hyper-drive while I hold them," he shouted.

Shey ran to the Nav-room.

He could feel the ship strain. Something was wrong. When Shey returned, Coz joined her.

He continued to hold off the other ship, while Coz forced open Tam's door. Within seconds, Coz, Tam and Shey returned to the open area, Tam in restraining cuffs.

"Did Danner set the hyper-drive?"

"No. It's not working," Shey said.

He pushed the pirate ship out as far as he could with his mind. "I'm going to check it below." He opened the lower hatch and climbed down the steps to the engine area. The hyper-drive was gone and the wires loose. He clenched his teeth and fists. Visually searching the area, he couldn't see the hyper-drive anywhere. He climbed up the steps and caught Tam's glance.

"What have you done with the hyper-drive?" He stormed over to where she stood, towering over her petite frame.

"I've been in my room. Why don't you ask Shey?" Tam glanced at Shey.

"Shey?"

"Why would I touch the hyper-drive?"

"Where is it?" He demanded Tam's answer.

"I told you, I've been in my room."

"Yes, guiding the pirates to our ship." Coz pulled Tam's restrained wrists up for him to see.

He reached out and ripped the ringlet off her wrist, breaking it, causing the red pulsing to stop. "You dare to accuse me of bringing the pirates down on us?" His voice grew deeper. A sound even he didn't recognize.

Tam clenched her jaw but didn't answer. Instead, she glared at him.

He held his hand out with the ringlet in his palm and called fire to burn the object to ashes.

Tam's eyes widened at the sight. "Huaca!" She called out

and tried to break free from Coz's grasp. Coz attached the restraining device to a chain and linked her to the ring on the floor hatch. "Your new quarters." Coz pointed to the chain.

Berto glared at Tam. He had heard the term huaca when he and Mariposa lived on Tarsius. He wanted to do something to Tam, but he controlled his anger.

"Tell me where the hyper-drive is and I'll spare your life," he said, squatting down to her level on the floor.

"I don't have it."

"No, but you know where it is."

"Why don't you ask her." Tam nodded in Shey's direction.

"Berto, I've been with you. You know I don't have it," Shey pleaded.

"I'll see if I can find it," Coz said, heading for the women's quarters.

He headed back down to the engine compartment and checked all the wiring. He found the comm wires cut loose that were fine when they left the station.

Using his tools, he spliced the wires together to secure them. Coz brought a small object down the steps.

"Is this what you're looking for?"

"Yes! Where did you find it?"

"It was in Shey's compartment."

22

———

Berto worked diligently wiring the speed enhancer into place along with the hyper-drive, while thoughts of the past few minutes ran through his mind. Of course, Shey had nothing to do with this. They were apart a few hours, but he knew better than to believe Tam. Tam was the one not to be trusted. He felt it every time he was around her. Yet the thought had been planted in his brain. Shey forgave him for her abduction, but still hadn't forgiven him for her brother's death.

The ship lurched, sending him to the floor. He pushed himself up and ran to the steps. Everything was ready. If he could get the Eligius away before the pirates connected, they would be safe. The ship jerked hard, and he fell off the steps. The hatch slipped into place. At the top step, he pushed the hatch but it wouldn't budge. Tam! He could use his powers.

"Everyone over here," he heard a muffled male voice say.

He waited.

"Raythun, take the Nav-room and secure it for towing."

Towing? There's no way they would tow this ship. He summoned his powers and blew the hatch straight up with his mind. He climbed up the last step, the hatch hovering near the ceiling. Tam hung over the side of the hatch by her restraints. One of the pirates clung to the top.

"Get me down from here!" the man shouted to his accomplices.

He slammed the hatch into the ceiling, Tam still hanging in place. The man wasn't so lucky. He left the hatch stuck in the ceiling.

"Well, if it isn't our old friend, Berto," Thadus said. "You had better have our ship, or those credits will be paid back tenfold."

"And if I don't have either?"

"Then I'm afraid your friends will die." He grabbed Shey by the arm and pulled her to him. "Starting with this one."

"I don't think so," he said, glancing at the three pirates in the room. He took quick aim at each man, starting with Thadus. He shot them with bolts of energy, knocking them across the ship and into the walls.

"Quick, get their weapons," Danner shouted. He grabbed some restraints and began using them.

Coz picked up the weapons while Shey checked them for hidden armament.

"Raythun, Thadus, come in," a voice called out over the dead man's comms.

"They'll be here any minute," Danner said, stowing the weapons in a compartment on the wall.

"Not if I can help it," he said, moving to the ladder that hung from the ceiling hatch. He pushed the pirate ship's hatch in place, sealing it with fire shooting from his hands. Then he slid Eligius' hatch in place, locking it securely. He moved his arms in a sweeping motion, using his mind to hurl the pirate ship farther out in space. After locking the ladder back, he turned to Danner. "Let's get this ship out of here!"

Danner and Shey ran for the Nav-room.

He pulled the hatch cover from the ceiling with his mind, lowering Tam to the floor. Coz fastened the pirates to a cable he ran through the ring in the floor hatch. "You forgot one," Coz said, dragging the dead man who had been squashed between the hatch and the ceiling. He and Coz stuffed him through the garbage chute.

"Care to join them?" Berto asked Tam.

"Is that how you killed my brother in Denoy?" Tam shouted.

"Your brother?"

"Yes! You hurled him against a cave wall. He died a couple days later from head trauma. My brother was fourteen. Don't you remember?"

He glared at her through narrowed brows. "The only boy I ever killed raped my sister when she was seven."

"That's a lie!" Tam shouted. "My brother would never have done that."

"He was a Chromian. Shey's brother. But your brother was one of two Tarsians who held her down, while the Chromian forced himself on her. If I hadn't stopped them, she would never be the same. I couldn't leave her sight for months."

"That's a lie!" Tam twisted in her chains. "My cousin saw the whole thing. Why did you do it?"

"The one I tossed against the wall was licking my sister's face while she screamed. They acted like animals, so I slung him against the wall like a piece of meat," he said. "I keep reliving that moment over and over in my mind. Tell me,

Tam, how well did you know your brother? Did he ever try hurting you like that?"

"You didn't have to kill him," she shouted.

"So, you wanted him to do that to other little girls?"

She turned away without answering.

"I didn't think so."

23

Berto rushed to the Nav-room. "You can use the hyper-drive now."

"Hang on!" Danner shouted, pulling the lever.

He and Coz fell against the wall in the Nav-room while the ship jumped to faster than light speed. Several minutes passed before he could move.

"Are we still on course for Persus?" he managed to ask.

"Yes. I did some course corrections before the jump. Is everything secured mid-ship?" Danner asked.

"As secure as we can make it. Our guests are attached to the ceiling hatch and Tam is attached to the floor hatch."

"Good. Next stop is the province of Izu. Now you two get some sleep."

Sleep was the last thing Berto had on his mind. He had entertained the thought that Shey still wanted revenge against him but it turned out to be Tam. Tam was behind all the sabotage on the ships. Tibu, well, he got what he deserved for killing Jans. Jans was a good man. He hoped he had seen the last of the pirates but he knew better. There were more of them out there. Without the tracker in his neck, he may be able to live a normal life, if there was such a thing. Tam's revenge surprised him because he didn't know she was Mendo's sister. Who else could be after him?

The memories of Mari clinging to him after the incident tore at his heart. If he hadn't left her alone when he interviewed for that job, Mari would have been safe. He had been tired of stealing to survive. He wanted to do honest work, to build a home for him and Mari, but he let Bordon talk him into stealing that cargo ship. Thanks to his own stupidity, he ended up working for Dram in a life of crime far worse than stealing food to survive. To top it off, he left Mari at that station on Tarsius. Did she find their aunt? Was Mari safe?

He tossed and turned until sleep overtook him.

"Hey, Berto? Are you awake?" Coz called from his upper bunk.

"Uh, no."

"It's our shift in the Nav-room," Coz persisted.

He pulled himself together, his mind foggy from lack of sleep. "I'm going to need some capu to wake up."

"I'll make us some," Coz said. He jumped from his bunk.

He checked on Tam, who slept on the hatch cover. She must be cold lying there. He went to her quarters, yanking a blanket off the bed and covered her with it.

Coz handed him a cup of beverage, raising an eyebrow.

"That was kind of you."

"Not really. I could have done it hours ago. I just didn't think about it."

He remembered Tam's wristlet. "I wonder..." He checked all the pirates for any wristlets, necklets, communicators, trackers, rings from fingers and ears as well as hair adornments. "Here's one," he pulled a communicator from a jacket.

"I didn't think about that," Coz said, joining the search.

Between them, they found three communicators and two wristlets. He burned the wristlets and destroyed the communicators.

"Good thinking," Coz said as they walked into the Navroom.

"How is the flight?" he asked.

"Uneventful," Danner said.

"We confiscated some comm equipment and destroyed it," Coz said, taking over for Shey.

"That's good. We don't want a repeat of our last adventure." Danner said.

"All our comms should be working now, too. Have you heard anything from the others?" he asked.

"Nothing. It was a quiet four hours," Shey said. "How's your neck?" She held him in place, checking the healing wrap.

"I forgot all about it," he said.

"It's healing nicely. No more bleeding."

"Sleep well." He winked at her.

"It's going to be a long four hours," Coz said.

Danner entered his quarters. Shey's door hissed open and she stepped into the room. She heard something, then turned around.

"You know they won't give up on you, don't you?" Tam asked her.

"I guess we'll have to fight them off," Shey said.

"What will Danner do to me?"

"That's up to the I.S.P. LE Danner will hold all of you as prisoners until we make it to Tarsius Station. But then, we may come across a prison ship before that," Shey answered. "You know, you sealed your fate when you called the pirates."

Tam hung her head and looked away. She tighted her fists against the restraints.

"I don't suppose Berto searched you?" Shey asked.

Tam jerked her head up and glared at Shey. "Don't touch me!"

Shey pulled her stun weapon from her holster and shot Tam on half stun. Tam fell over. Shey returned her weapon to it's place and searched Tam.

"Hmm." She pulled a cutting instrument from Tam's sleeve and found a lock release tool in her boot. She took Tam's boots and tossed them in their sleeping compartment then knocked on LE Danner's door.

"Yes?" Danner answered, opening the door.

"I thought you might like to see this," she showed the items to Danner.

"Where did you get those?"

"Our SM Recruit Tam has a hidden tallent. For our safety, I stunned her."

"Good thinking. Let the others know and get some sleep."

The door to the Nav-room hissed open. Berto and Coz jerked their heads in that direction.

"I thought you two might want to know what I found a few minutes ago," Shey said. She stepped between them and showed them the tools.

"Where did you get those?" Berto asked.

"Our teammate, Tam. I confiscated these after I stunned her. In the future, I suggest you search everyone for weapons. Male or female. She could have escaped and threatened all of us with her tampering of the ship." She handed the tools to Berto and left.

"Do you suppose we've seen the last of the pirates?" Coz asked.

"For now. We've eliminated all the possible communications devices." Berto studied the tools. He'd used similar items for stealing ships in the past.

"What if they have trackers, too?"

"That would be a problem. We don't know where to look unless they told us they had one or if the pirates activated them, like they did on me."

"They should be waking soon."

"We can keep them knocked out with a stunner. Do you want to do the honors?" he asked Coz.

"No. That privilege goes to you."

He got up and headed to his sleeping quarters to retrieve his stunner and put the tools away for safe keeping.

The pirates appeared to be waking, so he slipped into the galley where they couldn't see him. Tam slept on the hatch.

"Where are we?" one of them asked.

"Chained to an I.S.P. cruiser," another responded.

"Do you think the Captain can find us?"

"He'll be waiting for us."

"Shush! I hear something."

"He heard you, wombit!" Tam said.

"Thanks for the info, boys," Berto said. He shot each of them on full stun, along with Tam.

"Bad news, Coz," he said, entering the Nav-room.

"What is it?"

"They know our destination."

"How?"

"Either Tam told them or they tapped into our comm-links somehow."

"We haven't communicated with anyone, have we?"

"Not that I know of. I fixed the comms that Tam sabotaged. Maybe she communicated with them through her comm-pad before they found me through the tracker."

"We've got to get help," Coz said.

"Didn't LE Danner say there would be a cargo ship to pick up the slaves?"

"That makes sense. We couldn't put all those people on this cruiser. Maybe they only want the cargo ship?"

"No. They'll want their money back, too. They're out for revenge. We have to warn the others involved in this rescue, but I don't know who will be there."

"What's stopping us from using the hyper-drive and getting there faster than planned?" Coz asked.

"Not a damn thing!"

24

Hours later, a weak transmission broke through.

"...requests assistance."

Berto pressed the comm-link. "This is the Eligius. How can we assist you?"

"This is Adam Davis on The Guardian. We're being attacked by another ship."

"Adam? I thought you went back to Earth. This is Berto."

"Hey, Berto! Long story. We're on a mission to rescue slaves held by Taaka."

"What's your location?"

Shey and Danner entered the Nav-room.

"We got a transmission from The Guardian," Coz said.

"The Guardian? That's one of ours," Danner said, standing behind Berto's seat. Shey took over for Coz.

"Northern province of Persus. I'm sending you the coordinates now," a female voice responded.

Berto stood, letting Danner get into the pilot's seat.

"Is that who I think it is?" Shey asked.

"Genesis." Berto glanced at Shey. "They're under attack."

"By whom?" she asked.

Berto glanced at Coz. "Pirates," Coz said.

"Do you have a way to defend yourselves?" Danner asked, taking over the comms.

"Barely. They're using an ion cannon, ours was destroyed. We also have a cargo transport in place that's taking heat."

"Adam?"

"Yes. Danner, is that you?"

"Hey, man. We'll be right there."

Danner looked at Berto. "How did we get here so fast?"

"Uh, hyper-drive?"

"The pirates knew our destination. We got here as quickly as we could," Coz added.

"Berto, you and Coz take the weapons," Danner ordered.

Berto flew out of the Nav-room with Coz on his tail. The two of them shoved the hatch, with Tam attached, off the opening, and jumped down the steps.

Berto took the turbo cannon and Coz took the laser cannon.

"How's your aim?" Berto asked him.

"I'm really good in sims," Coz bragged.

"Let's do the most damage where it counts."

"You both strapped in?" Danner asked over the headsets.

"Yes. We're good to go," Berto responded.

"I'm sending the coordinates now," Shey said.

"I've got the ship in sight," Berto announced.

"I see them, too," Coz said.

A pulsing light came from the dark ship to their left, hitting the cargo transport. The shields protected them.

"I'm going for the guns," Berto said. He shot at the pulse's departure point. An explosion of light hit their vid-screens. Coz followed up with several shots before the pirates could recover. Berto caught a pulse of light coming from the planet below. He swung around with the cannon and aimed at the departure point, blasting several shots in the vicinity. Another explosion of light. He swung back around, picking up the pirate ship once more and shot at the exhaust vents in the back of the ship. "That ought to thwart their plans," he said.

"They're on fire!" Coz announced.

He checked his vid-screen. The pirate ship burned in two places. He aimed his cannon at the larger fire taking another shot.

"That ought to do it," he said.

The pirate ship began a rapid decent to the ground.

Coz took aim at another pulse of light coming from the planet, shooting a few times at the already damaged site, causing a final explosion. "Finishing touch," Coz said.

He and Coz high-fived each other.

"Great job!" Danner announced.

"Thanks, Danner and Berto! They disabled our laser cannon with the first shot. The cargo transport wasn't carrying weapons this time," Adam explained.

"We've got some catching up to do, Adam," Berto said.

"You got it, bud."

"Weapons check," Danner announced.

"All systems green," Berto said.

"We're going to land. Strap in, boys," Danner said.

He and Coz climbed out of the engine area. They slid the hatch in place.

"They won't let you off that easy," Raythun said.

"No doubt."

"Yes, the Captain will take what you prize the most," Thadus added.

"Let them try," he growled. Berto stepped into his

sleeping compartment, grabbed his stun weapon, and shot the prisoners and Tam, once more on full stun.

Inside the Nav-room, Danner spoke to Adam on the comm-link. "We'll be glad to assist you. That's our mission as well."

He and Coz strapped in to the extra seats behind the pilots' spots.

Danner set the Eligius down in a clearing. "Load up, team."

He and Coz each took a portable ion cannon. Danner and Shey took laser rifles. All of them took a laser weapon in their holsters.

Danner stepped out onto the hatch with Coz behind him.

Berto grabbed Shey as she was about to follow Coz, kissing her tenderly. She winked at him and he followed her down the ramp.

He closed and locked up the ship before bringing up the rear.

Danner communicated with Adam on his shoulder comm when Berto came up behind Shey.

"We'll circle around 90 degrees right. Adam and Genesis are going 90 degrees left. The transport team is going straight in," she whispered to him.

"What about the back?" he asked.

"There's another transport heading that way," she whispered.

Genesis called out their position over the communicator.

"That's the position of the—" A sharp blast sizzled over

their heads. He moved in front of Shey. "Pirates!" He slung the cannon onto his shoulder and blasted the location of the laser fire. Coz joined him, until another explosion ended the shots.

"We're being fired upon!" Adam called out.

Danner motioned for quiet.

He heard the sizzle of laser fire in the distance.

Danner pulled the scopes close to his eyes. "I see Adam," he whispered. "Fire two degrees right of that explosion."

He and Coz fired simultaneously at the location and another explosion went off. Within seconds, a few stray laser rifle shots sizzled past him.

"They're pretty good," Coz said.

"Too good," Danner said.

"The pirates are helping Taaka," Genesis said over the comm-link.

His research showed Taaka's fortress to be heavily guarded and well armed.

"Can you see the slaves?" Danner asked over the comms.

"No. We think they're inside the fortress," Adam responded.

"Can you see the fortress?" he asked out loud.

"All I see are trees," Coz mumbled.

"Shey, what do you see?" he called out.

No answer.

"Shey?"

His heart skipped a beat as he turned and saw Danner bent over—

"Shey!" He ran to her, setting the cannon down. He scooped her up in his arms, heart pounding.

"She has a pulse, but it's weak," Danner said. He clicked on his communicator.

He cradled Shey's body. "No!"

She reached up, touching his face. "I...forgive you, Berto. I love you." She slumped in his arms.

His heart ripped in two. He lay Shey down gently and stood up, facing the way they were headed. He called all his power and shouted in a voice he didn't recognize. "No!" A blast of energy flew out from him like a giant tidal wave, knocking over anything that wasn't buried in the ground. Trees bent or broke, boulders moved, people flew through the air, all in a matter of seconds. Then he did it over and over, sending wave after wave, moving toward the fortress. Nothing stopped him.

Coz followed cautiously behind him, carrying the ion cannon.

Berto stood outside the fortress. "Release the slaves now or be consumed in fire!" he shouted in that deep, disturbing voice.

He spied a couple of guards on the high tower wall taking aim. He raised his arm, shooting them with enough energy to knock them off the wall to their death. Then he hurled balls of fire at the tower, picking off anyone else still standing.

"Stop!" A shout from inside the tower. He waited.

The drawbridge lowered. Timidly, people came out, first a few, then small groups of them.

A cargo transport landed behind him. Coz, along with a couple other agents, helped the people board the ship.

Another cargo transport hovered over the fortress.

"Drop your weapons! All those who are not slaves, meet at the well in the center of the fortress," a voice announced over the intercom.

Slowly, other people came out of hiding. A group of I.S.P. agents with weapons gathered them up and loaded them onto the second ship.

Berto dropped to his knees. His heart broken, energy spent.

Out of the corner of his eye, he saw someone running toward him. He raised his arm to hurl another fireball.

"Berto!" A familiar voice.

He looked again.

"Hey, bud, it's me!" Adam said.

He froze. He almost killed his Earthen friend.

"You okay?" Adam helped him up. He gave him a hug. "It's good to see you."

He was numb. His heart stirred a little at seeing his friend again but he couldn't move. It felt as if he died inside.

"Great job!" Commander Howell came up and patted him on the back.

"That was awesome!" Adam said. "You should start with that next time."

"Shey's dead," he mumbled.

"What? No! She's alive. Gen's with her," Adam said.

"Genesis?" His heart lightened. "Shey's alive?"

"Yes!" Adam pointed behind him.

He turned and saw Shey coming toward him. His heart pounded in his chest. He ran to her, picking her up and swinging her around.

"I thought you—"

She kissed him firmly on the lips and he reciprocated.

"I believe everyone deserves a second chance, don't you?" Shey asked.

"Does that mean you'll be my mate?"

"Yes!"

25

Q *uinna Space Port, Planet Tarsius*

Berto, Shey, and Danner sat across from Coz in the Stellar Voyager Eatery & Lounge, waiting for Adam and Genesis to join them.

A pretty, dark-haired woman took their drink order and left.

"I saw her first," Coz said to Danner.

"Who are you talking about?" Berto leaned across the table toward Coz.

"That gorgeous woman over at the bar," Coz crooked his head in that direction.

Berto glanced where Coz motioned. "Excuse me," he said, standing. He headed toward the woman.

"Hey!" Coz leaned back in his chair.

"That's the second time he's done that to you, isn't it?" Danner asked.

Coz clenched his fists. "It sure is."

"Done what?" Shey asked, curious.

"Stolen his woman," Danner chuckled.

"Who was the first?" She asked.

Coz lowered his head. "You were, but he told me I wasn't your type."

"Oh, that's sweet." Flattered, she patted Coz' hand. "But I knew Berto long before I met you."

"Yes, but he didn't mention that until much later," Coz said.

She glanced toward Berto and saw him hug the woman at the bar. Then he kissed her cheek. Her happiness vanished.

Shey stood abruptly, knocking over her seat. "Excuse me," she said, heading toward Berto. He had some nerve.

"Uh oh," Coz mumbled.

Shey clenched her jaw. Berto better have a good explanation.

The woman pulled away first and glanced her way.

"Hello," Shey said as sweetly as she could, daring the woman to explain herself.

"Hi!" the woman responded.

"Shey! This is my sister, Mariposa. I haven't seen her in four anos."

Relief washed over her. "Oh, I am so glad to meet you!" She offered her hand.

Mari pulled her into an embrace. "I can see you mean more to Berto than a handshake," she whispered.

Shey glanced at Berto, raising an eyebrow. What exactly did he tell his sister? Mari pulled away to look at her. "Berto and I are very close," Mari explained.

Mari turned to a woman coming up behind her. "Kimber, take over for me today. This is my long lost brother." She waved her hand in Berto's direction.

"Sure, Mari," Kimber said.

Mari entwined her arms with Berto and Shey, walking them back to their table. Mari's happiness was infectious.

Adam and Genesis arrived, so Mari pulled up an extra chair, sitting next to Coz. Berto made the introductions, while Shey studied Mari's face. There was a deep resemblance between the two, but Mari was not quite as tall as Berto.

Berto filled her in on the past four anos, while Adam and Genesis added a few memories of Berto's fall off the cliff on Meta. Kimber brought the drinks before the stories began, but continued to keep the glasses full while they waited on their food.

"Berto and I both owe you for our lives, Genesis." Shey said, glancing at Berto, then Genesis. How could she ever repay her for that?

"A toast to Genesis," Berto said, lifting his glass.

Everyone lifted their glasses. "To Genesis," they said together.

Adam shared his story of how he realized he belonged with Genesis, while Kimber delivered the plates of food.

"Better late than never," Danner added. "Everyone knew you two belonged together but you."

"Yeah, I'm a little slow sometimes," Adam admitted.

"I love it when he changes color," Genesis teased. Sure enough, Adam's skin color turned pink.

"How do you do that?" Shey asked.

"It's a secret." Adam smiled.

Coz glanced at Mari while she watched Adam. "Are you staying in Tewa?" Coz asked her.

"You might say that." She smiled at him.

He cocked his head at her response.

"Actually, I live here at the Stellar Voyager."

"Mari, what did you do with all those credits I gave you?" Berto asked her.

"I bought this place and turned it into the Stellar

Voyager Eatery & Lounge. And now I have enough kashis saved to pay you back. Unless...you want to be partners?"

"That's tempting, but I'm committed to rescuing the slaves until everyone is found and returned to their home planets."

"Well, the offer is always on the table for you, Berto. You know that."

"I'll keep that in mind." He winked at her.

"When you four decide to go through the mating ritual, you can have the ceremony here at the Stellar Voyager. I love parties," Mari said.

Shey glanced at Berto then at Adam and Genesis. "I can get my father here in a few days." Excitement built within her.

"My family is already here," Genesis added.

"Our father was one of those abducted, Mari. He's at Tan Station, here on Tarsius."

"Our father? You mean he didn't abandon us?"

"No, he was abducted by Dram."

"I would love to see him," Mari wiped a tear with her finger. She stood up, glass in hand. "That's settled. We have the ceremony here in three days." She took a sip then sat down again.

"What if we have a mission before that?" Danner asked.

Coz wrapped his arm around Mari's shoulder. "I'd be glad to help you get everything ready," he said.

Genesis stood up. "I need to catch my family before they head back to Atria."

Shey stood up. "I'll go with you! I need to contact my father!"

"I'll take you up on that offer," Mari poked Coz in the chest.

"Did anyone hear what I said?" Danner asked.

Shey and Genesis headed for the Space Port's comm center.

Three days later, on the patio of the Stellar Voyager Eatery & Lounge, Vaedra was setting on the horizon. The colors in the sky were spectacular. The Eatery & Lounge sat on the lowest tier of the Quinna Space Port which hovered in mid-atmosphere and reached up into space over Tewa, Tarsius. Although the space port was completely covered in a clear dome, sunrises, sunsets, and the stars were breathtaking sights daily.

Berto and Shey stood together, holding hands. Beside them were Adam and Genesis. Mari had found a high priest willing to do the ceremony between mixed-race couples. She convinced the priest that the edict would soon be lifted.

Berto's father Alberto, Mari, Danner, Coz, and Shey's father Kaal stood to their left. To Genesis' right stood her father Malik, her mother Herda, and a new brother, Metik.

"You do understand that this ritual binds you for life?" the priest asked them.

"Yes, we do." Berto gazed into Shey's eyes.

"Yes," Adam and Genesis said together.

The priest raised his hands over the heads of each couple, praying. "May you each be blessed with longevity, health, prosperity, and fertility. Forgive each other their faults. Live in peace and love."

The priest then bound Shey's wrist to Berto's with leather cording. He moved to Adam and Genesis, binding their wrists as well. Then the priest took two white candles from the table and handed one to Shey, one to Genesis. On the table, another large white candle burned.

"Light your candles," the priest directed them.

Berto and Shey held their candle over the fire until it caught the flame. Genesis and Adam did the same.

"The leather cord around your wrists signifies the trials you will face in your new lives together. The candle signifies the hope and faith you must have to get through these trials."

The priest then handed each man a set of colored rings.

"Place the ring on your mate's finger," he instructed.

Berto placed the smaller ring on Shey's mid-finger. Shey placed the larger ring on Berto's mid-finger. Adam and Genesis did the same.

"The colors stand for longevity, health, prosperity, fertility, peace and love. You will remain bound together in love. I declare you as mates to these witnesses. Live long, love well, and prosper."

Everyone cheered and clapped.

Berto and Shey blew out their candle and shared a passionate kiss.

Adam and Genesis blew out their candle, but Adam tilted Genesis backward and kissed her tenderly on the lips.

Afterward, Mari's friends played music throughout the evening, while Berto and Shey managed to dance together with their wrists still bound.

As they danced around the patio, he heard Danner and Coz discussing something. He moved Shey closer.

"I thought recruits couldn't fraternize with officers?" Coz asked.

"Technically, SMST Berto is an officer, so it's all good."

Book 3 Betrayed

Chapter One

PLANET EARTH

Washington, DC

Was it wrong to pray that nothing happened every day?

Keely McGuire sat in the back of the briefing room while Gowan went over assignment changes. She prayed her assignment stayed the same. She had been at the White House a year now and still felt like a rookie. Gowan had finished talking and hadn't called her name. She must be in the clear. While other agents got up to leave, she headed to the front of the room to check her assignment. Gowan spoke to another agent away from the desk. She ran her finger down the page. Good. She was assigned to the Oval Office today.

A heavy hand rested on her shoulder. She straightened and turned. Gowan.

"Yes, you still have Oval Office duty."

"Thank you sir." She managed to say.

"I'm surprised McGuire."

"Oh?"

"Most agents look forward to a change in duty at least every now and then. Sometimes they even ask for a change, but not you. Why is that?"

"I like where I'm at, sir."

"Do you, McGuire?"

She swallowed hard and nodded. She couldn't get away fast enough. When she got to the Oval Office, she straightened her bullet-proof vest and checked her holster to make sure her Sig was in place. She didn't care that other agents got promotions or moved into other assignments. She liked where she was. It was safe.

When her shift ended, she offered another prayer of thanks for an uneventful day. She checked her watch. Her parents had invited her over for the weekend. She hadn't seen them in a month and looked forward to the visit.

Her cell phone rang as she got into her car.

"Hello David, how was your day?" She asked.

"I got a new lead on a story I've been working on. How about you? Did you wear that new ring I bought you?"

"My day was quiet as usual. I'm sorry, but I forgot to wear the ring. I promise I'll wear it next week."

"Good. Be sure that you do. I just can't believe you work at the White House and nothing ever happens around there."

"I'm sure things happen there, I'm just not at the scene where it does."

"Is this the weekend you're heading into Virginia to see your parents?"

"Yes. Would you like to join me? I'm sure they'd love to meet you."

"Maybe some other time. I'll be hanging out with the boys this weekend. You have fun. I'll see you when you get back."

Keely set her phone in the seat next to her then pulled off her vest. She had been careful not to mention to David she was a Secret Service Agent. Although they had been seeing each other for nearly a month, she didn't feel comfortable sharing what her career entailed, especially since he worked for a local newspaper.

It was probably good that he decided not to take her up on her offer. Her mother didn't like him and she hadn't even met him.

She put the top down on her convertible and pulled her hair loose from the tight bun she wore while she worked. Since she had packed her bags earlier this morning, she headed south to Virginia. This weekend she had to tell them she was having second thoughts on her career choice.

Virginia Countryside

Keely McGuire stared through the eyepiece of her father's telescope. It sat on the back deck of the house, facing the moon on a cloudless night. She enjoyed spending time with her parents in the quiet countryside, away from the hectic pace of Washington, D.C.

"What am I supposed to see, Dad?" His sudden interest in star gazing surprised her since his only hobbies were fishing and hunting.

"Just look at the moon long enough and you may see a flash of light shooting out." He stood a few feet away and coached her.

"Yeah, I just saw one! What is it?" A pang of excitement

hit her as the powerful telescope enabled her to see the flash.

"I think they're UFOs."

Keely straightened. "Really?" She shoved her hands into her jeans pockets. A shiver ran down her spine. She had never heard her father speak about UFOs.

"I think there's something going on there. I mean, it's a perfect location for aliens to visit Earth."

"If there were aliens on the moon, the astronauts would have seen them." She dismissed his argument and moved to one of the seats on the deck and sat down. Her father joined her. It had been years since she had discussions like this with her parents.

"I think they did. Haven't you ever wondered why they stopped going to the moon?"

Keely studied her father. His red hair, mostly gray now. And the twinkle in his blue eyes had gone out. "I thought it had something to do with funding."

"No. That's the BS they fed to the public. I saw a video where an astronaut spoke to a group and said they had a space force."

"Yes, the president said he was going to start a space force." She recalled a news conference not long ago.

"Keely, this was in the 1960's. We've had a space force for over 50 years now."

Mrs. McGuire brought out some coffee and put it on the coffee table where Keely sat. Her auburn hair was dusted with gray and her green eyes had lost their sparkle as well. When did all this gray hair happen? Why hadn't she noticed before now?

"If we've had a space force for 50 years, why haven't we been told?" Keely asked. She stirred some cream into her coffee.

This conversation was getting interesting but it started a nervous twitch in her stomach.

"It's a matter of national security," her mother said. She sat across the table from Keely and her father. "The government wouldn't want wide-spread panic."

"The government has denied the alien landings since Roswell and then reversed themselves by feeding us disinformation for years," her father said.

"Why are you two suddenly interested in UFOs?" Keely sipped her coffee.

"Because we've seen one," her mother said.

VAEDRA SYSTEM, PLANET VESTRA MAJOR

Inside the Council of Nations building

Lieutenant Tremol stood before the small group gathered around the table in Vestra Major's Councilor office. The circular room with large windows sat atop the Capital City's largest building. The view of Sentinel City was breath-taking.

Wearing the dress white uniform of the I.S.P., Tremol cleared his throat.

"Gentlemen, thank you for coming on such short notice."

"Why are we here?" Admiral Esrith demanded. He, too, wore the dress whites, but those of the space military.

"I've come to ask for your participation on a goodwill mission to Earth." He paused to let that sink in and hopefully gain interest.

"Earth?" Councilor Thebes of Vestra Major asked.

"Yes. Earth is a planet in another system that we in the Vaedra System have used for centuries to relocate our people of mixed races."

"Yes, I know what Earth is," Thebes began. "What goodwill mission are you talking about?"

Tremol turned to Adam Davis, who sat beside him at the table. "Adam?" The Earthen who had been mistaken for the criminal, Dram, had become a friend. He hoped Adam could win them over. After all, this was Adam's idea. The group was already showing some interest.

Adam stood and he sat down.

"When I was abducted and taken to your system, I realized how far advanced your people are compared to us on Earth. I was hoping to get your government to send some Ambassadors to our government on Earth and share technology. We could share what we have with you as well." Adam glanced around the table.

"Why should we do that?" Admiral Esrith asked.

"Earth would be a great ally in times of war," Adam said.

"We haven't had a war in decades, thanks to our military," Esrith answered. "We do fine on our own."

"Allies are great in times of war or peace." Tremol stood.

Esrith was going to be a tough sell. He patted Adam on the back. "There is more information that we could exchange with the people of Earth, not just military prowess. Think of the science or medicine we could exchange." Tremol noticed some Councilors perk up.

"I think it's an excellent idea," Councilor Contor of Tarsius said. "It could open up all sorts of trade business for every planet."

Councilor Tal of Persus chimed in, "We could trade our precious metals from our mountains."

"Perhaps the Earthens would trade with us for our silk," Councilor Shim of Vestra Minor asked.

"This is great! Does that mean you'll come to Earth?" Adam asked, standing.

"I need your vote of approval to move forward on this mission. I've already cleared it with my supervisors of the I.S.P." Tremol explained.

"What has the Interplanetary Space Patrol got to do with a goodwill mission to Earth?" Esrith asked.

"As you know, Admiral, the I.S.P. is the first line of defense in our system for law and order. If things escalate, then we call in the military. Sharing this with the Earthens would be essential for them to move to a space capable military if they don't already have one."

"Are you getting a promotion out of this?" Esrith asked, crossing his arms over his chest.

Tremol tensed his jaw. He knew this was coming. "If all goes well, I hope to get a promotion, yes. But this would elevate all the planets in their standing as far as trade goes. Wouldn't all of the planets benefit from more trade?"

"Yes! We could all use more business. Count the Tarsians in," Contor said, standing.

Tal stood. "Count Persus in as well."